LAWFULLY *Held*

Elle E. Kay

Faith Writes Publishing
266 Saint Gabriels Rd
Benton, PA 17814

ISBN: 978-0-9994856-2-0

This book is dedicated to the dogs who have impacted my life.

Introduction to The Lawkeeper Series

There's just something fascinating about a man wearing an emblem of authority. The way the light gleams off that shiny star on his badge makes us stare with respect. Couple that with a uniform hugging his body in just the right way, confidence, and mission to save and protect, it's no wonder we want to know what lies underneath.

Yes, what echoes deep inside those beating hearts is inspiring. Certainly appealing. Definitely enticing. Although those ripped muscles and strong shoulders can make a woman's heart skip a beat--or two--it takes a strong, confident person to choose to love someone who risks it all every day. Anyone willing to become part of a lawkeeper's world might have a story of their own to tell.

The undeniable charisma lawmen possess make all of us pause and take note. It's probably why there are so many movies and TV shows themed around the justice system. We're enthralled by their ability to save babies, help strangers, and rescue damsels in distress. We're captivated by their ability to protect and save, defend the innocent, risk their lives, and face danger without hesitation. Of course, we expect our heroes to stay solid when we're in a mess. We count on them for safety, security, and peace of mind. From yesterday to today, that truth remains constant.

Their valor inspires us, their integrity comforts, and their courage melts our hearts--irresistibly. But there's far more to them than their courageous efforts. How do they deal with the difficulties they face? Can they balance work and life? And how do they find time for love outside their life of service?

We want to invite you on a journey--come with us as we explore the complex lives of the men and women who serve and protect us every day. Join us in a fast-paced world of adventure. Walk into our tight-knit world of close friendships, extended family, and danger--as our super heroes navigate the most treacherous path of all--the road to love.

The Lawkeepers. Historical and modern-day super heroes; men and women of bravery and valor, taking love and law seriously. A multi-author series, sure to lock up your attention and take your heart into custody.

Visit The Lawkeepers on Facebook:
https://www.facebook.com/TheLawkeepers/

Join our mailing list:
https://lawkeeperseries.com/newsletter

The Lawkeepers is a multi-author series alternating between historical westerns and contemporary westerns featuring law enforcement heroes that span multiple agencies and generations. Join bestselling authors Jenna Brandt, Lorana Hoopes, Elle E. Kay, Patricia PacJac Caroll, Evangeline Kelly, Ginny Sterling and Barb Goss as they weave captivating, sweet, and inspirational stories of romance and suspense between the lawkeepers -- and the women who love them.

The Lawkeepers is a world like no other; a world where lawkeepers and heroes are honored with unforgettable stories, characters, and love.

** Note: Each book in The Lawkeepers series is a standalone book, and part of a mini-series of sorts, and you can read them in any order.

Chapter 1

After looking around to be sure they were alone, Justine unhooked Lindy's leash. The German Shepherd contained her excitement and heeled beside her waiting patiently to run off and search for the hidden object. A hand signal and verbal command freed Lindy to take off down the trail. The dog lay down at the foot of a prickly pear cactus to indicate she'd hit on something. Justine pulled out a toy and they began a spirited game of tug of war. They moved along at a comfortable pace until a hawk broke the silence with a piercing squeal about two miles into their hike.

"Come on, Lindy, girl, you ready to head back to Grandma's house?"

A low bark answered her.

They turned and ran back in the direction they'd come. Justine gradually slowed her steps a half-mile from the car to give them both time to cool down. By the time they reached her mother's Buick LaCrosse, they were both breathing normally.

She opened the driver's door and Lindy hopped in and moved to her usual spot. The drive to her mother's was quick.

After unlocking the door, she pushed it open. "Hi, Mom! We're back."

"Who is it?" Her mother rounded the corner a blank look on her face.

"Mom, it's me, Justine. Your firstborn, remember?"

Another blank look.

"Come, let's have some dinner. Okay?" She gently put an arm around her mother and led her to the kitchen.

The visit wasn't going to last as long as she'd like. Her unit expected her and her partner back in Virginia. She was already three days into a seven day leave. How was she going to put her mother in a home? The woman who'd taken care of her until she'd left home for college. How could she fail her like this? Maybe she could bring her to Virginia. No. That wouldn't work either. Her sister and brother also had demanding jobs. This was the only way. Being the eldest, the responsibility fell on her.

Justine chopped the capers and added them to the bowl of ground beef. She used to leave them whole, but her nephew picked them out. He thought they looked like deer poop. Chuckling to herself at the thought of someone actually adding deer poop to meatballs, she stuffed her hands into the gooey mixture and got started mixing and forming them.

Thirty minutes later she pulled the pan from the oven and added them to the sauce. Justine preferred to call it spaghetti sauce, but it was her grandmother's recipe and she'd referred to it as gravy. They'd had it translated from the original Italian after she'd passed away.

"Mom, do you think Grandma Gillespie, would approve of my meatballs and gravy?"

"You mean, my Joseph's mother? Why don't you call and ask her?"

"I'll do that, Mom." It was easier than telling her once again that Isabelle Gillespie had passed on ten years earlier.

Brady poured the half and half into his coffee and frowned when it curdled. After dumping it down the drain, he poured another cup. He took a sip of the bitter black liquid and opened the paper. A cold nose nudged his hand. He looked over at Blitz' bowl and saw it was still full of kibble. "What do you need buddy?"

Blitz walked to the door and waited. Brady slowly stood putting the paper back down. Apparently, Blitz was ready to start the day. He grabbed the canine's leash from the hook by the door and opened the door for the dog. He locked up behind them and opened his truck. Blitz hopped inside wagging his tail wildly. If only Brady enjoyed going to work half as much as his partner did. He grinned at the dog as he started up the engine. Ten minutes later they arrived at the station. He liked his job, and having a partner like Blitz made the days enjoyable, but some mornings he woke up wondering if he was missing out on something important. Today was one of those days. Brady glanced at his watch and saw he still had time for a cup of coffee with decent creamer. He let Blitz out and they trudged inside.

Fitz was standing at the coffee pot when he walked into the break room.

"Fresh?" Brady asked.

He held up the thick black sludge in his cup for Brady's inspection. "It's from this week, I think."

"I'll make a fresh pot. The creamer was bad at home. I need a decent cup of coffee."

"You don't need creamer. Drink it like a man."

"I'm secure enough in my masculinity to take creamer in my coffee, but thanks, Fitz."

"What's on the agenda for today?" Brady emptied the filter bin and reached for a fresh filter from the cabinet above the coffee maker.

"Not much. Some paperwork to chase down after the murder suicide last week and the bomb threat hoax at Morrisville High."

"No new crazies overnight?"

Fitz shook his head. "I wouldn't count on the sanity continuing."

"I rarely do." Brady turned the machine on and watched as the liquid began to run into the pot. He went to the refrigerator and took out the creamer inspecting the date before adding some to an empty mug.

"Shouldn't you be taking yours to go?" Fitz asked.

"Not if I have to finish the paperwork from the Morrisville High hoax."

"You were on that one?"

"One of several troopers backing up the DPS Police Officer on scene."

"Get that to me pronto and head out. I have a bad feeling about today."

"I hate it when you say that." Brady poured some coffee into his cup of cream and walked to his desk.

Twenty minutes later he and Blitz were piling into their silver and black Ford Interceptor SUV.

Justine's morning was not going smoothly. They had to be around somewhere. She'd left them on the night stand, same as always. Her mother must've moved them. She glanced at her watch. There was no time to continue the search. She'd look again when she got back from the nursing home. If she didn't find her credentials by afternoon she'd report them missing. Oh, how she hated the thought of doing so.

She swept her hair into a ponytail, put her Glock in her hip holster and grabbed her purse.

Her heart was heavy as she drove to meet the director of the senior care facility. Leaving Lindy with Mom seemed like the best thing to do. Mom needed her more than she did, but she longed for her canine's company as she drove the last few miles to the Sunshine Canyon Assisted Living Home. It was such a beautiful name. Too often the names of these facilities didn't match the reality.

A few minutes later, she pulled into the lot, it was actually quite beautiful. The named seemed to fit. She parked the car, but didn't get out. Instead, she laid her head down on the steering wheel and closed her eyes. Maybe prayer would help. She hadn't been praying much lately. God hadn't answered her prayers to heal her mother or if He had, He'd said no. She tried to understand but couldn't. This was hard. Why this particular trial so soon after they'd lost Dad?

Less than five minutes later, she opened the door to the home. A receptionist sat behind a wooden desk reading a novel. A sign-in sheet sat on the corner of her desk. The woman, who appeared to be in her mid-fifties, looked up from her book and smiled. "May I help you?"

"Yes, please. I'm Justine Gillespie. I have an appointment with Margaret O'Donnell."

The woman stood as she spoke. "She's waiting for you. You can follow me."

An elevator ride and several turns later she was being ushered into Ms. O'Donnell's office. A cramped room with only one tiny window.

"If you need me to show you the way out, have Margie buzz me and I'll be back in a jiffy."

"Thanks, but I think I have it."

"Have a seat, Ms. Gillespie. Do you want coffee?"

"No, thanks. I'm fine."

"Let's get started, shall we?"

"Sure." Justine felt her hand move to her hair as if to twirl it, a habit she'd broken ten years earlier. She forced her hands to stay folded on her lap.

"Why don't we start by you telling me about your mother?"

"Okay." The meeting took well over an hour. The woman asked thoughtful questions and showed compassion and understanding for Justine's dilemma.

She toured the facility and was satisfied with it. The institutional smell bothered her, but it was the antiseptic odor many such facilities had. She made arrangements to bring her mother on Saturday. Her heart was breaking, but there was no better option. At least her mother would be safe here.

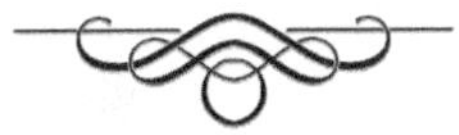

Brady scratched behind Blitz' ears while they cruised Interstate 10. Blitz was the best partner he'd ever been assigned. He never argued or complained, was loyal, and did his job better than most. The German Shepherd was a multi-purpose asset capable of apprehension and detection.

He pulled up behind a Buick LaCrosse on the off-ramp. The driver slowed, but didn't stop at the stop sign. It happened frequently since they'd only recently changed it from a yield to a stop. He stayed behind the Buick as it approached the traffic light. The driver sped through without so much as a tap of the brakes. "What do you think, Blitz? Should we pull her over?" He turned his lights on and followed. She didn't notice him. He considered the possibilities. The driver could've been drinking or using drugs. She could've had a medical emergency.

Finally, she slowed and pulled over to the right. He pulled up behind her and ran her plates before stepping out of his vehicle and approaching the driver's-side window.

The sound of sirens broke her out of her reverie. She glanced in her rear-view mirror and saw the state police SUV. She pulled over, fully expecting it to pass on. Instead, it pulled off behind her, lights flashing.

The trooper came to her window.

"Ma'am, is there any particular reason why you ran a red light back there?" He removed his sunglasses as he spoke.

"What red light?" She raised an eyebrow. The trooper had a touch of green in his golden brown gaze.

"The one just past the off-ramp from I-80." The deep gravelly quality of the trooper's voice made her want to keep him talking.

"I didn't see it. I'm sorry." She could see he had dark hair under his trooper hat, but couldn't get a good look at him.

"License and registration, please."

She reached into her glove compartment, but her wallet and her credentials weren't there, then she remembered. They were somewhere at the house. Glancing at the seat beside her, she realized she'd left her purse at the nursing facility. She opened her window the rest of the way and handed the officer the registration for her mother's Buick. "I'm sorry, I left my purse at the nursing home. My wallet is inside it."

"One moment. I'm going to run this."

He returned a few minutes later. "This registration doesn't belong to you. The vehicle belongs to a Hilda Gillespie. We'll need to verify you have permission to drive it."

"That's fine. She's my mother. I'm Justine Gillespie."

He left her sitting in the car for another ten minutes before coming back to her window. "Mrs. Gillespie says she has no children and didn't give anyone permission to drive her car. Ma'am reach your arm out the window and open the driver's door from the outside. Then put your hands on the hood of the car."

"Are you serious?"

"Yes, Ma'am. Do it now."

"My mother has dementia. You need to speak with her

nurse. Her not being able to identify me is not unusual."

"Do as you were requested."

"Fine, but you have no idea what you're doing." She did as he asked releasing herself from the car, then placing her hands on the hood.

He read her her rights. "Do you have any weapons or anything sharp that might poke me?"

"Yes. I have a Glock on my hip and a Sig Sauer in the glove box."

He secured the weapons and walked her over to his car. As he did so, she told him. "I'm Special Agent Justine Gillespie, FBI. I'm in town to visit with my mother."

"I'm going to take you in. We can verify your identity at the station."

"You don't have a computer in your car you can use for that purpose?"

"Like I told you earlier, you have the right to remain silent. For heaven's sake, please do so." He shut the door before she could respond.

Justine closed her eyes and counted to ten. This was so not her day.

FBI. Unbelievable. The woman was interesting if nothing else. She had to be loony to think she was some sort of super special agent or whatever she'd said. Perhaps she was off her medication. There was a sadness in her eyes. A haunted look. Common in career criminals. They wanted to stop but didn't know how. Maybe he could get her some help. It wouldn't take much time to get this sorted out once he got her back to the station. He'd find out who she was. Reaching over he scratched behind Blitz' ears. The shepherd provided a calming presence.

He looked back at the woman in the car. Her dark hair was half in and half out of her ponytail. The outfit she wore looked like professional slacks and a short-sleeved dress shirt, but they were askew and had paw prints. It looked liked Blitz had chased her down. He wondered what institution the woman might've escaped from. If she wasn't a career criminal, she must be a deranged mental patient.

It didn't take long for them to make it to the station. He took the woman out of the car and led her inside. "We'll get this straightened out right quick and get you back on your way, if you're telling the truth." He chuckled, sure she wasn't.

"And what about my mother's car?"

"We'll have it towed. Can't release it to you when the owner says she didn't lend it to anyone."

"Great. Fabulous."

"Watch the sarcasm, Miss."

The feisty brunette rolled her eyes. Definitely not an FBI agent. The woman couldn't control her emotions in the slightest. She would be a ticking time-bomb for any agency. He led her to holding.

"You are not seriously considering leaving me in here?" She growled the words.

He nodded and sauntered away to run the information she'd given him. The internet connection was slow. The rest of the country might have high-speed data, but they were a bit behind the times in the sparsely inhabited desert lands of southwestern Arizona. What passed for DSL here, was not in the same league as what they had in Phoenix.

Trooper John Kearney walked toward him holding up what looked like a black leather wallet. "Hey, can you run this while you're at it. I've got a security officer from the power plant in my office. Found it on patrol."

"Run it yourself."

"Aw come on. I'm due to get out of here. A hand, please."

"Fine."

"The security dude said there was a bomb threat called in at the plant. When he saw this, he thought maybe something happened to the agent assigned to investigate."

"I didn't hear about a threat."

"Me neither. Maybe they contacted local."

"Yeah. Maybe, but you'd think we would've been kept in the loop. I'll check this out. A sigh escaped when he opened the credentials."

"Something wrong, Brady?"

"I locked up a federal agent."

"No way. The chick on the credentials?" A huge smile spread across John's face.

"Don't call an FBI agent a chick. What's the matter with you?"

A booming voice interrupted. "Conference room. Now."

They shuffled into the room. Brady spoke. "What's up, Fitz?"

"Bomb threat at the power plant. We're going to recall troopers from patrol and call in as many people as we can."

Brady exchanged looks with John Kearney as they listened to the briefing. According to Fitz this bomb threat happened an hour and twenty minutes earlier. Shortly before he'd brought in Agent Gillespie. As soon as Fitz finished speaking, Brady stood. It was time to get her released.

"Where are you going?" Trooper Kearney asked.

"To eat crow and beg forgiveness."

The other trooper chuckled.

Brady approached the holding cell cautiously. "Agent Gillespie. Please accept my sincere apologies."

"It's Special Agent. So, you've verified my identity. I'm sure you could've accomplished that in the field."

"I thought I should bring you in considering the vehicle owner's claims."

"I'm glad you take the word of an elderly woman with dementia over the word of her lucid daughter."

"You didn't appear so lucid at the time. And it's not my fault you lost your credentials in the desert."

"No. It's not." She put her hands on her hips. "Wait. Back-up. How do you know I lost my credentials?"

"An employee from the plant brought them in about the same time I was bringing you in."

"Did you call it in?"

"I take it you didn't report them missing?"

"No. I should have, but I thought I'd misplaced them in the house. I didn't realize I'd actually lost them. Did you call it in or not?"

"No. I recognized your scowling face when Trooper Kearney handed me the credentials. After the briefing, I came back here to apologize."

"Am I free to go?"

"Yes, of course." He ran his fingers through his hair. "I should call it in, you know."

"Yes. You should." She poked him in the chest with her index finger. "You should've cleared this up in the field too, so how about we call it even and you leave well enough alone."

"I'm okay with that." He handed her back her credentials.

"How can I get my mother's car back?"

"I didn't have it towed yet, but we do need to verify you have permission to drive her car."

She rolled her eyes. "Are you serious with this? I'm here to put her in a home. She can't remember who I am more than half of the time."

"I'm just doing my job, but obviously you are who you said you are, so I don't doubt you about the car. I'll get your mother's car towed back to her house. Sorry about the mix-up."

"You are a serious threat to my sanity."

He chuckled.

"What's so funny?"

"My first impression might've been that you'd already lost your sanity."

"Nice." She grinned.

"Hey, can I ask you something?"

"Sure, but I may not give you an answer."

"How did your credentials end up by the power plant?"

"I train my dog on some of the remote trails near there. It's only a few miles from Mom's house. I must've lost them when Lindy and I were playing."

"Lab?"

"German Shepherd."

"I'm surprised you didn't mention yours when you saw Blitz."

"I was rather preoccupied with being detained."

"I thought FBI only used so-called gentle dogs like Labrador retrievers." He walked slightly in front of her, so she could follow.

"Lindy was brought to us from another agency. Her extraordinary talent suits our needs well."

"So, you weren't here to investigate the bomb threat at the power plant? I didn't think it was possible for the FBI to be on scene so fast."

"There was a bomb threat?"

"Sure was."

"How long ago?"

He glanced down at his watch. "If the security guard's statement is accurate, about an hour and a half. Shortly before I brought you in."

"I need to call in. My purse is still at the nursing home. My boss has been trying to reach me."

"How do you know that?"

"There was a bomb threat in my hometown, at the largest nuclear facility in the country, while I'm in town. There is no doubt in my mind he's been trying to reach me."

"You can use the telephone in the conference room. Follow me."

Chapter 2

"How do you know about the bomb threat if you didn't get my voicemails?" SSA Harrison Reed asked in his usual gruff manner.

"From a state police trooper." Justine finger combed her hair. "It's a long story. What do you need from me?"

"I need you to get back to that nursing home and get your work cell."

A sigh escaped. "Okay. After that?"

"Jackson and Bruce are on their way out there. They'll catch up with you when they land. In the meantime, secure the scene and report back to me within the hour. This needs to be wrapped up by the close of business."

She dropped her head. Clearly her boss didn't understand distances in this part of Arizona, but she wasn't about to argue with him. She'd find a way to get it done by recruiting local help, starting with Trooper Brady Hall. She'd give him something better to do than detaining innocent people.

She hung-up and dialed her mother's house. She spoke with the home-care nurse, Rita, to let her know she probably wouldn't be back until late. She stuck her head out of the conference room door.

"Hey."

Brady walked toward her.

She stepped out of the room. "May I have my weapons back now?"

"Oh. Sorry. I'll get them."

"I guess you had time to log them in?"

"I'd get my badge taken if I hadn't."

"Fair enough. Would you hurry? My boss is fuming."

"Does he know about me bringing you in?" Brady visibly cringed as he said the words.

"Not yet."

"What's his problem, I thought you were supposed to be on vacation?"

"I am, but I'm always on-call. He expects me to answer at all times."

"Must be a pain."

"At times. Yes, it is." She took out her ponytail holder and ran her fingers through her tangled strands. "I'm going to need a lift."

"Sure. I'll get you a ride."

"No. I'm going to need assistance. Take me to see Sergeant Sean Fitzpatrick?"

"You want to see my boss?"

Justine nodded.

"Okay. Follow me."

She followed him a few short steps to an open office door. Brady blocked the doorway. "Sergeant Fitzpatrick. I have Special Agent Gillespie to see you."

"It's about time. Send her in." He stepped out of the way and whispered as he walked past her. "Good luck."

"I was expecting you more than an hour ago." He barked.

"I'm sorry for the hold up," she looked pointedly at Trooper Hall. "I'm here now."

Once the door shut, Sergeant Fitzpatrick sat back down. "Let's get down to business. Have a seat." He indicated the only empty chair in the office.

"I don't have time to sit. I need a few things from you." She matched his direct manner and asked for what she needed including a car to go to the nursing home, backup at the power plant, and Trooper Hall's services.

"Fine. Whatever you need."

"We'll get a perimeter set up and go from there."

"Fine. Get going then."

Justine left his office shaking her head. This day kept getting better and better. It was time to pick up Lindy and get to work.

"Let's go." She spoke the words as she walked past Trooper Hall.

"I need to check with Fitz."

"I took care of it. You're with me." He handed her back her weapons one at a time.

"First order of business is to send someone else to the nursing home to get my bag."

"Fitz agreed to that?"

"He agreed to help with whatever the FBI Bomb Squad needs."

"And you're with the FBI Bomb Squad?"

"You betcha."

"I arrested a super special agent."

"A what?"

"Private joke."

"We need to get moving. There's no time for bad jokes."

"My bad. Come on." He signaled for Blitz to come and they moved silently to the parking lot.

"Sorry buddy, but we got a ride-along." He opened the back door and the shepherd jumped in.

Lindy jumped out of the car, excited to be getting to work. Justine made her way inside the original perimeter the local and state authorities had set around the plant. The Maricopa county sheriff stood by a large saguaro cactus with a group of other officials. He was wringing his hands like the world was coming to an end. Justine couldn't blame him. If the bomb threat was real and couldn't be diffused or contained, then for the residents of Wintersburg, Tonopah, and the surrounding areas, that might be a reality. Special Agent Marc Jackson stood behind her, his canine, Bruce, at his heel

She met with the security officer who received the threatening phone call. His supervisor stood over his shoulder, a silent presence. Whether he was there to calm or threaten his employee, Justine couldn't say. His behavior seemed off, but then again, some people weren't good around others. She'd always thought she fit in that category.

"What time, precisely did the call come in?" She'd read the file on the way, but asked the question to see if there were inconsistencies in the man's statement.

"11:33 ma'am.

"Precisely?

The man nodded.

Did you recognize the voice on the telephone?" Special Agent Jackson interjected.

"No."

Justine hurried to where the sheriff and his cohorts were standing, motioning for Brady to join them as she did. Jackson followed closely on her heels. Brady lifted the rope to join them on the inside, but she shook her head. "You will do us far more good out there coordinating the efforts to secure a new perimeter. Besides, if a bomb is found, we're going to need you out there."

She looked from the sheriff to Brady. "We're going in. While we execute our plan, we need you to move the perimeter out another five miles. While most bomb threats are hoaxes, we can't take any chances, especially considering the target is a nuclear facility. If we find something, we'll have you set off the emergency sirens before we send in the wheelbarrow."

"A wheelbarrow?"

"It's what they call the robots. I'm going to ask you to take this threat seriously. We should have more information for you shortly." Justine once again made eye contact with Brady and the sheriff before turning back to Jackson. By silent agreement, they walked toward the complex.

As they approached the door of the first building, Marc spoke. "If we get out of here alive, drinks are on me."

"You know I don't drink."

"Yes, I know. Coffee and pie?"

"We'll see. Let's get out alive first." She followed the dogs in. It had been a couple of hours since she'd last reported to SSA Reed. She wanted answers quickly, so she could pass them along. The country would be on edge if this was real. Terrorism was the first thought that came to mind. She hoped it was a hoax.

The dogs walked out ahead of them, clearing rooms one by one. They quickly cleared the first building and moved on to the second. In the second building, it didn't take Lindy and Bruce long to sniff out explosives. They were materials that belonged on-site and were not intended for harm.

Moving along, the dogs began a search of the expansive outdoor area concentrating on the area between the cooling towers. Lindy hit on something suspicious. She laid down near a lunch box. Justine recalled Lindy. Marc put his hand on her shoulder and they stared at it for a moment. So innocent looking. Someone's lunch, set aside until break-time.

Justine let Marc take her hand as they made their way back beyond the inner perimeter to the FBI box truck Marc had picked up at the Phoenix field office. Once inside they suited up and brought out their portable x-ray machine.

It wasn't unusual to find bombs. They'd diffused over fifty of them together, but a bomb at a nuclear power plant. This was new. It could be a disaster of epic proportions. It wasn't like setting it off in the middle of a major metropolis, but it would render this area uninhabitable.

Justine picked up the her cell. Her first call was to SSA Reed. He'd be briefing the Director of the FBI, who would in-turn brief the Acting Secretary of Homeland Security and she would brief the President. Justine's next call was to Trooper Brady Hall. She should probably be calling Seargent Sean Fitzpatrick, but had a feeling Trooper Hall was up to the challenge. Besides she wouldn't mind hearing his deep voice one more time. There was a chance she wouldn't be going home, but she forced the thought from her mind and sent up a prayer.

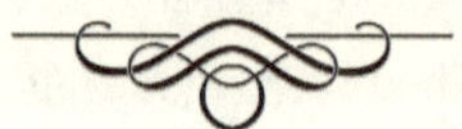

Brady answered his cell. "Trooper Brady Hall."

"We need to evacuate the area. We found the device. I think we'll be able to diffuse it with our wheelbarrow, but you should evacuate everyone in case we run into a problem."

"That kind of problem would blow you and your partner to smithereens, wouldn't it?"

"Most likely."

"How about we avoid that scenario?"

"That's the plan. Look, we don't want widespread panic, but you're going to need to sound the alarms."

"Fitz isn't going to like it."

"I'm sure he's not, but it's better than seeing a nuclear plant go kaboom near towns full of civilians."

"It sure is." He rubbed his temples to alleviate the pain beginning to throb there. "I'll get it done. Stay safe."

"God willing."

He thought it odd that she would say those words, but it somehow seemed fitting coming from her. The day replayed itself in his head as he made his phone calls. Moments later the sirens were going. He knew from previous testing they could be heard more than fifteen miles in every direction. There would be widespread panic unless people thought it was a drill. The radio and television announcements informing residents that "this is not a drill" would kill any chance of misunderstanding. A few minutes passed as he stared toward the inner perimeter where he knew Justine Gillespie and her bomb squad friend had gone with the dogs.

Justine Gillespie was a study in contradictions. Cool under pressure, but crazy disorganized at the same time. There was something about the disheveled dark-haired beauty he found captivating.

He hadn't considered dating a career woman. He'd always thought it would be nice to marry one of the quiet girls he'd met at church. The ones who wanted to homeschool children and take care of the house. There weren't many one income families around anymore, but he thought when he found an exceptional woman, they would make it work. Unfortunately, the women he'd found so far, weren't even close to fitting the bill, so he remained alone. Maybe what he thought he wanted wasn't what he wanted at all. He forced thoughts of the FBI agent from his mind and started making telephone calls, starting with Seargent Fitzpatrick.

The heat inside the ninety pound protective suit was stifling. Every time she put it on, Justine questioned her career choice.

She sent up a silent prayer as she and Marc slowly and cautiously approached the device to x-ray it.

The tension was palpable. She was afraid to breathe. When they finished x-raying the device they moved back beyond the inner perimeter again and she finally took the time to breathe normally.

They took out the wheelbarrow, known affectionately to them as Stan the robot man. Marc controlled the robot remotely as Stan disarmed the bomb and sprayed it with acid to render it power-less.

A rush of emotions followed the deactivation of the device. Marc threw his arms around her and for a brief moment, she allowed the contact and then she remembered and pushed him away.

"What's wrong, doll?"

"Nothing. I don't think we should be so close is all."

"Oh, come on. You're not still mad, are you?"

"I wasn't mad. I simply ended a relationship that had no hope for a future."

"Because I didn't want to get married? Seriously, what kind of wife would an agent make?"

"And what kind of husband would an agent make? We both know what we want and it isn't each other."

He sighed. "There's always going to be one person you can't walk away from even when you know you should. You're that person for me."

She shook her head and kissed him on the cheek. "In that

case, I'll do the walking away. We have reports to submit."

"What about the coffee and pie?"

"Rain-check?"

"You're not getting out of it that easily."

"Fine, but we're going to have to invite the guys from the DPS to join us. I need someone to take me home."

"I can take you home."

"I'm not sure I want you to know where my mother lives."

"You're funny."

"Let's invite them anyway. It'll be fun." She'd prefer to avoid being alone with Marc, but didn't want to hurt him. "I'll call Brady and ask him to let the others know."

"Brady? Not Trooper Hall?"

"If you knew the morning we'd shared, it wouldn't surprise you. I'll fill you in over dessert, but you're going to spring for real food too."

"You're on."

Justine picked up the telephone and dialed Brady.

After one ring, Brady picked up. "Trooper Brady Hall."

"Stan the robot disarmed it. Call off the alarms."

"Praise the Lord. Glad you're safe."

The words caught Justine off-guard. She'd expected him to be happy that she and Jackson were still alive and the bomb was diffused, but she hadn't expected him to say those words. Praise the Lord. Simple words, but packed with power. Had he meant them? Was he praising God or were they nothing more than empty words to him? She wanted to know the answers, but didn't plan to ask him the questions.

"Hey, Brady. Do you and your team want to grab dinner and coffee with us?"

"I'm in. I'll have to check with the others."

"Let me know how many. We're going to call ahead."

"Give me five minutes and I'll have a head-count from our end."

She brushed the hair off her sweaty forehead. "We'll be waiting."

It was only three minutes later he called to let her know Seargent Sean Fitzpatrick, Trooper Marguerite Kinicki and Trooper John Kearney would join them, but Trooper Bob Masters had to get home to his pregnant wife who needed a chocolate marshmallow milkshake and some caramel popcorn.

Justine let the restaurant know the count and got in the truck. "Marc?"

"What's up, doll?"

"Please stop with the terms of endearment."

"Okay. What's up, agent?"

"I think you could leave off the agent too. Call me Justine."

"Picky today, aren't you?"

"Just frustrated that you can't treat me like you treat everyone else."

"Doll, we dated for six months. You're not everyone else."

"I know, but we have to work together. Would you, at least, try?"

"If you insist." He lifted her hand to his mouth and kissed it.

"Not helping."

He stared out the windshield as he turned onto Route 11. A muscle in his jaw twitched. "What is it you want to discuss?"

"Never mind." She had wanted to ask him to treat her with civility and professionalism in front of the state troopers, but decided to let it go. Why did she care? It wasn't as if he ever veered into the inappropriate around others. Yet, she didn't want him to display his usual sense of possessiveness. It shouldn't matter. She'd probably never see these people again. For some reason, Brady's smiling face was seared into her consciousness. She couldn't concentrate on anything else, least of all the man who sat beside her. The same man who'd joined the marines thinking it would relax him and the FBI Academy to keep him in shape. He didn't have a need for down time. Marc Jackson moved at warp speed with no pause button, except when it came to relationships. She admired his profile as he drove. He was a ruggedly handsome man. His fierce protectiveness and slight neediness might be attractive to some women, but not to her. He was eye candy and she could easily stare at him for hours,

but they didn't mesh as a couple. They wanted different things out of
a relationship. He would make some woman a fabulous husband.
She wasn't that woman.

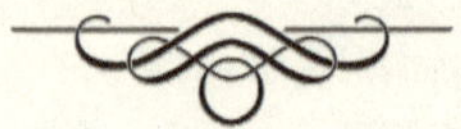

Once inside, Justine took a moment for her eyes to adjust to
the dimness. Looking around, she met the eyes of the hostess.

"Reservations?" The woman looked at the dogs with dis-
taste.

"Yes. For Six. Gillespie."

The hostess grabbed menus and motioned for them to follow. At the table, Marc pulled out a chair for her and sat beside her.

"That woman is not a dog person." Justine whispered.

"Clearly not." He pulled his chair out and sat. "How long
until the rest of our party arrives, doll?"

Justine narrowed her eyes to slits and glared in his direction.

"Sorry. I forgot." His soft laughter betrayed the lie.

Before she could respond the hostess came back with the
rest of their party. Fitz and Marguerite sat to the left of Marc, leaving Brady to sit to her right with John Kearney at his right. Justine
tried to meet Marguerite's gaze, so she could make a crack about the
testosterone in their party, but the woman already had her eyes
glued to the menu.

"Another day, another bomb diffused." Marc sipped his water.

"I don't know how you do it. Aren't you scared?" Marguerite asked him.

"Not really. It's my job." He put down the water glass.

"He's lying." Justine interjected.

"How do you know?" Marguerite asked.

"I do the same job. He's lying. You can't help but be scared when working with explosive devices. Even if we weren't scared for ourselves, we'd be scared for our canines."

"I guess that makes sense," The other woman said.

Brady lifted his glass of water. "A toast to the FBI sending us the best of the best to prevent a catastrophe out here on the outskirts of nowhere."

"Well, the best of the best weren't available, so SSA Reed sent the best of the mediocre." Justine raised her glass. "I was already here, so that only includes Special Agent Marc Jackson. With me, you got the best of the best."

"Funny, doll." Marc took another generous swallow of water.

She cringed.

Marguerite stood. "I'm going to powder my nose. Would you care to join me?" She made eye contact with Justine.

Justine was not the type who went to the restroom in pairs, but she didn't want to offend Marguerite. "Sure." She rose and started toward the back with the other woman.

When they reached the restroom, Marguerite cornered Justine. "What's up with you and the hunk?"

"You mean, Marc?"

"Yes, Marc. I noticed he called you 'doll'. Are you involved with him?"

"We dated, but we've moved on."

"Okay. Perfect. So, you don't care if I go for it?" The woman pulled a tiny bottle of perfume from her purse and applied it.

"Not at all." Justine freshened her lip gloss. She could taste Marguerite's perfume and wanted to gag. She dug in her purse for a hair brush and concentrated on brushing her hair. After a few seconds, she turned back toward the other woman. "Is Brady single? I noticed he doesn't wear a ring." Heat burned her face. She couldn't believe she'd asked the question.

"He sure is."

She was sure the whole restaurant would notice her flaming cheeks. When they arrived back at the table Marguerite smiled coyly as she deliberately brushed up against Marc on her way back to her seat. It took every bit of self-control Justine could muster to keep from laughing out loud.

"So, Marc, I promised to tell you more about this morning's adventures."

"Yes, you did. The reason you were so cozy with Trooper Hall."

"Exactly." There was a twinkle in Brady's eyes.

"I was driving along Route 11 on my way home from a tour

of a nursing facility, minding my own business."

"Running a red-light." Brady interjected.

"When out of nowhere comes this silver and black SUV with lights and sirens going. I assumed he was going around me, since there was no reason for him to pull me over."

"Except for that running a red-light thing." Brady added.

"Then the guy pulls up behind me. Imagine my shock." She opened her eyes wider.

"And when I pull her over, she is armed and dangerous, driving a possible stolen car with no identification."

She laughed. "I was a wreck."

"Yes, you were." Brady grinned.

The laughter was contagious. Marc laughed until tears filled his eyes. Fitz let the corners of his mouth turn up slightly. They were clearly enjoying the story.

When those events were recounted successfully, Marc told some war stories and Marguerite talked about a particularly hairy stop she'd made when she'd first started patrolling.

Brady placed a hand on Justine's arm to get her attention. The electricity that surged through her body alarmed her. It wasn't the first time he'd touched her. He'd arrested her that morning. It was hard to believe it had been so recently. It felt like she'd known him much longer. She looked up at him trying to gauge if he'd felt the same electric shock she had.

"Can I offer you a ride home?" He asked.

"I'll take her home." Marc interrupted.

"Marc, don't you need to get back to Phoenix with the truck."

"No rush. I can take you."

"Okay. Thanks." She didn't say anything more. If she did it would be too obvious that she wanted to spend time alone with Brady.

Marguerite stretched herself out like a cat. "Marc, I need a ride back to the station. If you'd let Brady take Justine home, then maybe you could give me a lift."

Marc looked around at her co-workers and raised an eyebrow. "Sure. I guess."

Justine found it funny how dense Marc could be. It was so obvious to anyone else that the gorgeous Marguerite was flirting with him, she could catch a ride with anyone of her co-workers. Marc didn't recognize her tactics. She'd never understood how someone could be highly intelligent and clueless at the same time.

Chapter 3

"I'm glad I got to bring you home." Brady looked over briefly before returning his gaze to the road. "You are?"

"Yes. I want to make it clear how sorry I am about this morning."

"Oh. That." Justine tried to quell her disappointment. She'd been hoping he was glad for another reason. Why was she doing this to herself? She'd be leaving town in a matter of days.

He drove down the road and pulled into the drive at her mother's house. "How'd you know which house?"

"Registration, remember?"

"Yes. I remember." A deep sigh escaped.

He met her gaze. Lifting his hand to her hair, he lowered it as if he'd been burned. "I'm going to ask you something, and if I'm completely out of line, you can smack me or punch me, whatever."

"Not the best start to a question." She wondered what was going on in his mind. He seemed as nervous as she felt.

He swallowed. "I'd like to take you out. On a date."

"Okay. I'd like that. Only problem is I'm only in town for a few more days."

"How about tomorrow night? Will you be able to get someone to stay with your mother for a few hours?"

"I think so. She has great nurses taking care of her. The service can usually get someone. Today's lack of notice probably didn't make for a happy nurse, so we'll see."

"Can you let me know in the morning?"

"Absolutely." She smiled, relieved he shared her interest, but disappointed it couldn't go anywhere.

"Thanks for not punching me." He brushed the hair off her face and leaned a little closer.

"Don't thank me yet. I'm leaving my options open." She reached for the door handle. Lindy stood up. Blitz sniffed at Lindy's butt before lying back down.

"I guess it's no use asking you to let me open the door for you?" Brady asked.

"I've got it tonight, but tomorrow night, I'll wait for you to open all doors."

"Thanks. My ego requires it." He chuckled.

"Goodnight, Trooper Hall."

"Goodnight super Special Agent Gillespie."

Once inside the house, Justine stood at the door and relished the feelings coursing through her. It couldn't possibly work between them. She lived in Virginia. He lived in Arizona. They both had careers. It couldn't work. It wouldn't work, but tonight she wanted to forget logistics and simply enjoy the feeling of having an attractive man want to take her out on a date.

She moseyed into the kitchen and found the nurse cleaning up.

"I'm sorry about today, Rita. The bomb threat turned out to be real."

"I know. It was all over the news."

"How was Mom today?"

"It wasn't a good day for her. She hasn't been well this week. She had one decent day last Tuesday, but the rest have been challenging."

"I'm sorry I wasn't here to help. Mom is the reason I flew out here, but I couldn't ignore today's incident." Justine didn't mention being detained by the state troopers. If Rita had answered the telephone that morning, the situation could've been averted, but then Justine might not have gotten to know Brady Hall. Who knows if Fitz would've assigned him to the power plant case if she hadn't specifically requested his assistance. She sent up a silent prayer of thanks for Marguerite. If she hadn't distracted Marc, Justine would be sitting in the truck at this very moment arguing over his desire to revive a relationship better left to die a quiet and peaceful death.

"Do you need anything else before I go?" Rita asked.

"No. Thank you again. You are appreciated."

"You be careful, Miss Justine. I saw you on the news today. Your mother needs you. You should find a safer job."

"Thanks, Rita. Drive safely."

Justine looked in on her mother. Hilda Gillespie seemed so peaceful when she slept. She wished more than anything she could turn back the clock for her mom. She'd been a strong independent woman and had raised her to be the same, but now she was forced to depend on others. People she couldn't remember from one day to the next.

Brady and Blitz arrived home after a five-mile run. Sweat ran down Brady's back and he leaned against the counter to catch his breath before jumping in the shower. When the telephone rang, he answered on the first ring. "Hello." He briefly wondered if answering on the first ring made him look desperate.

"It's Justine Gillespie."

"The caller-ID informed me." He sat down at the kitchen table and picked up his coffee mug.

"And you still decided to answer. Interesting."

"Were you able to get a nurse to look after your mother tonight?" Another sip of hot liquid soothed his nerves.

"Yes. Are you sure about this?"

He chuckled. "I am."

"If you say so."

"Dress casually. I'll pick you up at six, okay?"

"You have to give me more information than that. How casual?" she asked.

"Jeans are great. Hiking boots are perfect."

"Are we going for a hike?"

"In the dark? It's a thought, but, no."

"A man of mystery."

"I'll see you tonight. Hope your day goes well.

"Right back at ya." He ended the call and stood to put the cordless phone back on its base.

Blitz was getting antsy, pacing back and forth in the kitchen. Brady leaned over to give his dog some love. The canine ran off and brought back his favorite toy. They played as hard as they worked and Brady needed to release some pent up tension, so he and Blitz tugged at the toy until it was time to get ready for work.

Brady hurried off to shower and shave. Fifteen minutes later, he was loading Blitz into the truck. Tonight would either be magical or a complete disaster, but he'd find out if Justine Gillespie was his kind of girl. The thought made him smile.

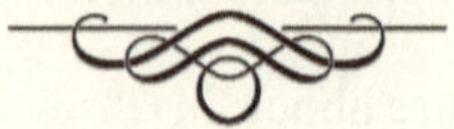

Justine laced up her hiking boots. She'd dressed in a cream-colored top paired with the only jeans she'd packed. She toyed with the idea of adding some hoop earrings, but didn't want to look like she was trying too hard. She checked out her outfit in a full-length mirror and decided she needed a belt. After adding some lip gloss and mascara she joined her mother in the den.

Brady wasn't due to arrive for another twenty minutes. She would spend time with Mom while she waited. It had been a particularly good day for her mother. She'd had more lucid moments than usual and Justine wanted to savor these precious minutes.

Settling down on the couch beside her mom, reaching over, she patted her mom on the knee. "Are you sure you don't mind me going out? I could always send him home when he gets here."

"Don't do that. You'll end up an old-maid like your Aunt Vivian."

"But, Mom, we're having such a nice day together. I should stay."

"Go. Have fun." Her mother drained the last of her milk. "I'm going to bed soon anyway."

It was true, but Justine wanted to somehow find a way to extend the time she had with her mom. "Mom, I love you."

"And I love you, but I won't be around forever, you're going to need to get married, so I won't have to worry about you."

It wouldn't occur to her mother that Justine might not want to marry. Justine had been doing a fine job of caring for herself. Her work paid the bills and let her save for the future. It was fulfilling and exciting. Yet, there was a tiny part of her hoping for more. She wanted what her mother wanted for her. A family of her own.

A gentle knock on the door interrupted Justine's thoughts. She rose to answer it.

"Hi." Brady stood there looking relaxed and handsome in jeans and a flannel shirt.

"Hello." Justine held the door open for him to enter. "Give me a few minutes to talk to my mother's nurse. I'll be back in a moment." She left him standing in the foyer.

"Rita, I won't be back late. Call if you need anything."

"Go. Have a nice time with that handsome young man. Hilda will be getting washed up for bed soon. You won't miss much around here."

"Thanks again, Rita. I'll see you in a few hours."

"Go! He's waiting."

"I'm going. Bye."

The twinkle in his eye made it clear Brady had overheard her conversation with the nurse.

"Don't get too full of yourself, Brady. You're not that handsome or that young."

"Aw, come on now. Be nice."

She laughed.

Her full-throated husky laugh did something to Brady's insides. It made him want to tell her jokes to keep her laughing. Sadly, he didn't know many jokes.

"You ready for this, Special Agent Gillespie."

"Maybe you should call me Justine."

"Nah. I like the sound of Special Agent. How many guys living in the Mojave desert manage to get a super special agent to go out with them."

Another laugh. He could see himself falling for this woman.

True to her word, she waited while he opened the front door and then again while he opened the passenger door of his truck.

"What are Lindy's plans tonight?" He asked as he settled into the driver's seat.

"She's planning to sleep at my mother's feet until I get home. Although she claims to be disappointed Blitz didn't invite her on a date."

"I think he'd like that. We'll have to set them up."

"So where are we going Trooper Hall?" She turned her body toward him as she asked.

"You can keep calling me Brady."

"Not if you're going to call me Special Agent."

"Fine. Justine it is then." He'd never known a Justine before. It seemed to fit the woman beside him.

"You didn't answer the question."

"What question?"

"Where are we going, Brady?"

"You'll see."

Twenty minutes later, he pulled onto a dirt road and then a long curving driveway lined with post and rail fencing. "Where are we?"

"My ranch."

"Oh. What are we doing at your place?"

"You'll see."

"You say that quite a bit."

"I do. Don't I?" He grinned.

He opened her door and led her up the trail beside his old ranch house. "It's not really hiking, but it's uneven terrain, hence the request for you to wear hiking boots."

"I'm glad I listened." She breathed in deep, enjoying the earthy scent.

"Me too. Otherwise, we'd have been stuck at some stuffy restaurant on this beautiful evening."

A full moon gave them the light they needed to get there, but when they reached the pasture, he took her by the hand and led her to a blanket he'd laid out before going to fetch her. She looked around enjoying the mountain views all around them. A complete picnic dinner was set out, including a bottle of non-alcoholic sparkling cider.

"How did you know that I don't drink alcohol?" She sat down folding her legs under her.

"I didn't. I don't drink. And I love sparkling cider." He poured her a glass and handed her a piece of fried chicken.

"Really?" She took a bite of the chicken and reached for a napkin.

"Yes. I drank some when I was younger, but found it was rather unsatisfying."

"Same." A gentle breeze ruffled her hair.

When they'd finished eating, Justine let herself relax and lie down on the blanket. Looking up at the night sky she marveled at the beauty. She couldn't see the stars when she was home in Virginia. There was too much light. Seeing the sky lit up with millions of stars reminded her of her childhood. She'd missed it during the years she'd been gone. This was what life was supposed to be about, wasn't it? Moments like these.

"Can I ask you something?" she asked

He leaned down over her, and she met his gaze in the moonlight. "Anything."

"Do you believe in God?"

"Absolutely. How could anyone look at the beauty of a night sky and not realize it had been created by a master craftsman?"

"Good question. But, I was asking on a more personal note. Yesterday when you learned we'd diffused the bomb, you said 'Praise the Lord.' I wondered if it was just something you said or if you'd meant it."

"Of course I meant it. I'd been praying for your safety and you were safe. How could I not praise the Lord for answer to prayer?"

"Thank you. It meant a great deal to me."

"You're welcome. Now it's time for me to ask a question."

"Okay."

"Are you seeing that guy you work with? He seemed to treat you like more than a friend."

"We were more than friends, but we broke it off. I care a great deal for him, but we aren't meant for each other."

"Are you sure? I don't want to get in the way."

"I'm sure, but I don't know if it matters. It's not like you and I can make anything work with you living here and me in Virginia. I only have a couple more days. Not that I need to be thinking about making a non-existent relationship work after one date. I'll stop babbling now."

"God works in ways we can't always understand and if we are meant to become something more, He'll help us make it happen."

"Thanks, Brady. I like that thought. I'll leave it in God's hands and enjoy the time I have with you tonight."

He leaned down close to her, his lips a fraction from hers. "May I kiss you, Justine?"

Her breath stopped and anticipation coursed through her. "Please." It was a gentle kiss. A sweet kiss. It left her wanting more. She resisted the urge to pull him down to her.

They stayed there watching the stars for a long while before he stood. "I guess I'd better be getting you home."

"I suppose so. Thanks for this. I can't imagine a more perfect date."

"I'm glad you liked it. I'd love to have you come back in the daylight to meet the animals."

"That would be amazing."

"Are you free tomorrow?"

"You betcha."

"Then it's a date. I'll pick you up at eight o'clock a.m."

The drive back to Justine's place was a quiet one. Brady wasn't sure if her silence was a comfortable one, a thoughtful one, or if he'd said too much. Maybe he'd moved too fast asking her to see him the following day. He clenched the steering wheel tighter and let his breath out slowly. He sent up a prayer asking for peace and acceptance whatever happened between him and Justine.

When they arrived at her driveway, he pulled in and parked. Justine looked over at him. "Do you want to come in for a cup of coffee."

"I would, but I don't want to disturb your mother."

"You wouldn't. She's a sound sleeper, but I do have to go in and send the nurse home."

"Okay. If you think it's all right, I'll join you for coffee."

Justine led him to a sunroom off the kitchen. He heard her as she spoke quietly to the nurse, thanking her for staying. A minute or two later, he heard the front door close before Justine reappeared with pastry on a plate.

"It's a day old, but it was the best I could do at such a late hour." She set the tray down on an end table.

"It's perfect. Thanks."

"The coffee will be ready in a minute."

"Are you nervous or something?"

"No." Her fingers twirled her hair.

"I'll behave. I promise."

She laughed that husky laugh of hers and he thought it might undo him ruining his gentlemanly intentions.

"The coffee's probably about ready. I'll be back in a jiffy." She hustled off to get it.

He watched her go, admiring the fit of her jeans. It would take a miracle for Brady to keep his intentions pure around this woman.

She came back with two steaming mugs. "Do you need

cream and sugar?"

"Cream if you've got it."

Justine hurried off again only to return moments later with a ceramic creamer. So much more classy than a paper carton, but also completely unnecessary.

"You didn't have to go to so much trouble. I'm fine with the half and half container."

"The nurse puts it in that. I wouldn't dream of being so re-fined." She laughed again.

Her laugh would be his undoing.

"Thank you for the coffee. Will you sit down and relax now?" He added the cream to his coffee before leaning back and attempting to make himself comfortable on the wicker loveseat.

"I'll try. I don't have a lot of men over. Especially not at my mother's house."

"I don't bite." He smiled. "Unless of course, you ask nicely."

Another laugh. He reached for her hand and held it while they sat quietly and drank their coffee.

Twenty minutes passed in silence. He lifted her hand to his lips and kissed her palm. His eyes searched hers for an answer to an unspoken question. Leaning over he waited for her lips to part and he kissed her. It started out controlled, but soon his fingers were tangled in her hair and he was kissing her with a passion he knew could get them both in trouble.

He broke off the embrace and held her at arm's length. "As much as I want to continue this, I'd better go before I lose control.

Are we still on for the morning?"

"We are." She cleared her throat and tried to smooth down her hair.

Justine watched as Brady pulled out of her driveway. Her fingers moved to her lips. She still felt a tingling sensation. It was something she'd never had with Marc. Electricity set her body on edge with anticipation. She stood there at the door for several minutes after his taillights had disappeared from sight.

She slowly made her way up the stairs to her childhood bedroom. After brushing her teeth and dressing in comfortable pajamas, she picked up her Bible to read a few chapters before going to sleep, but thoughts of Brady's lips on hers kept her from concentrating on the words. She laid her Bible back down on the night stand and tried for prayer instead. "Lord, I don't know what's going on here, but I lift it up to you and ask for your will to be done. Father, please help me do what's best for Mom. You know her needs far better than I do. If I'm wrong about the home, would you help me figure it out. In Jesus' precious and holy name I pray. Amen."

Even though she didn't know how God would answer her prayer, she felt better having talked to Him. He knew what was best for her life and her mother, so she would trust Him with it.

Lying down, she drew the covers up and snuggled into her pillow. Thoughts of Brady's kisses filled her head as she attempted

to fall asleep. After twenty minutes of tossing and turning, she finally turned on an audio book to distract her mind and keep her from
focusing on the sexy trooper.

Chapter 4

He was impressed when Justine was waiting at the door. He'd arrived promptly at eight o'clock. He was used to dating women who believed men should have to wait for them while they finished getting ready.

She jogged out to the truck. "Is it okay if Lindy joins us?"

"Of course. Blitz will be thrilled for the company." He looked back at Blitz as if to confirm.

Justine hurried back inside and came back out with Lindy in less than a minute. She had the speed of someone who had trained with her dog for countless hours. Once outside she waited for Brady to come around and open the passenger door.

A woman who was prompt and appreciated gentlemanly gestures. What more could he ask for? Would it be pushing his luck to hope she didn't mind getting a little dirt on her clothes and hay in her hair? He laughed to himself at the picture he had in his head of her feeding the animals. He'd find out soon enough how she felt about getting a little crud on her jeans.

The drive back was passed with small talk. When they pulled up at his ranch house, he parked by the barn. He'd unloaded the bales of hay from the trailer earlier, but hadn't fed the critters yet. He'd waited, so she could see all his animals as they fed them. He thought they'd start with the rabbits and end with the horses. His usual routine.

"You ready to meet everyone?" He asked. Blitz jumped down and ran up to her. He was ready to show her his domain. When Justine let Lindy out of the truck, Blitz forgot all about Justine and ran off with Lindy.

"I'm ready, but I think Lindy and Blitz have ditched us."

"Good for them. It's their day off too."

He took Justine by the hand and led her to the rabbit hutches. "Meet my bunnies, Scarlet, Sarah, and Skye." He took a bag of vegetables from his pocket and put some in each cage. "We'll get them some hay and fresh water, but we need to go inside the barn. Do you think you're ready for that?"

"Sure. Why not?" She shrugged her shoulders.

He laughed out loud knowing what was about to happen. He opened the gate and led her into the barn.

Three goats jumped on her before she took two steps. As she walked past the horse stalls, Bella grabbed a hold of Justine's hair. She looked up into the deep brown eyes of the Chestnut mare and grinned. Stroking the mare, while trying to knock down the goats, she turned back to face him. "It must be gratifying to have so many friends to visit with every morning."

He chuckled. "It is. I grew up near the city. There were ordinances that prevented us from keeping livestock. When I moved out here I purchased the ranch, I can't run it myself and work full-time, so I have some help, but I love it. This life is refreshing."

"What brought you out here?"

"The Arizona Department of Public Safety stationed me out here. It became more of a home to me than Phoenix ever was. I'm happy here."

"That's obvious." She bent down to play with a goat and another one jumped on her back. The sound of her laughter filled the barn.

His relief was palpable. This girl was what all the others hadn't been. She wasn't afraid of animals or getting dirty. He'd brought her here last night to test her. Another relationship with a prima donna was not something he wanted. He needed someone real. Who wasn't afraid of a little dirt or a little bomb for that matter. The woman couldn't be more perfect. God would find a way to work this out. If she was the woman for him, God would make a way.

Justine relished the sensation of her hand in Brady's as they relaxed on the swing and watched Lindy and Blitz take turns chasing each other. It was a hot day for early March, having already hit ninety degrees. Earlier in the week they'd had beautiful seventy degrees temperatures. The weather had been fickle since she'd arrived in town. Her phone buzzed in her pocket, so she pulled it out to see who was calling. Marc. She would ignore it, but it might be work-related.

"It's Marc. I have to answer in case it's about work." She got off the swing and walked a short distance away, so she could concentrate on the call.

"What's up?" she asked.

"I'm rejoining you in Arizona, doll face."

"Why? Another bomb threat?"

"Apparently, yes. A school this time. Reed thinks it's a credible threat."

"He wants you on it now."

She sighed. So much for her time off and the hope of spending some time with Mom. "Why didn't Reed call?"

"He's planning on it. I wanted to give you a head's up, so you could be on top of it when he does call. He's currently coordinating with state and local authorities."

"Okay. Thanks for letting me know. Would you email me the file? I'll get right on it." She disconnected the call and hurried back to the swing.

"It looks like we're going to have to bother you for a ride again." Justine lifted an arm and Lindy came running. "Apparently there is another bomb threat in the area and since I'm already here, I've been assigned to work it."

Her heart was heavy. Normally she loved the excitement of her job, but today, she wanted to live. To sit here another hour with Brady and then spend a quiet afternoon with her mom.

"You're going to spend your life running off into dangerous situations, aren't you?" Brady's voice was barely a whisper.

She muttered back "That's always been the plan." For the first time ever, she wondered if the plan needed some adjustments.

Brady got to his feet and called Blitz back from herding the goats. A moment later they were taking off in the truck.

Justine's hopes that the bomb threat was a hoax designed to provoke an early dismissal on a Friday vanished when Lindy hit on explosives within minutes of entering the building. After a visual inspection, she determined it wasn't safe to wait for back-up and for Stan the robot man to arrive. She was going to have to go in, unless they were able to coordinate with well-equipped local authorities. Her best hope lay with DPS bomb squad, they'd already provided her with the EOD suit she was wearing. It was slightly lighter than her usual one, making walking somewhat easier. She hoped they'd have a robot and some personnel available to assist in bomb dispos-al. There wasn't time to wait for Marc to arrive.

Picking up the phone, she dialed SSA Reed and apprised him of the seriousness of the situation. After confirming the area had been evacuated, she was instructed to stay back and await fur-ther orders. He would touch base with the Arizona Highway Patrol and get back to her.

She hadn't been waiting long when she was knocked off her feet. The explosion was deafening, shaking the ground with violent force. She tried to sit up, but felt like something was sitting on her chest. Her movement was severely restricted by the weight of the bomb suit and whatever was holding her down. Her ears rang and her vision faded around the edges.

Brady lifted the flag pole off of Justine and dragged her from the rubble. He removed her helmet and leaned close to feel for her pulse.

"She's alive!" he yelled to Fitz, who'd arrived in time to see the explosion.

Fitz hollered into his phone. "Where are those paramedics? They should be here by now."

Seconds later, Brady heard the sirens. "Hang in there, princess. The cavalry is on their way." The paramedics pushed him out of their way as they removed her bomb suit and loaded her into the ambulance. He hopped inside the ambulance to ride with her.

Fitz walked up to the back of the ambulance. "Where are you going? I need you here."

"She needs me more than you do. It's still my day off."

"You've got it bad for her, don't you?"

"I'm quite fond of this woman. Her mother has dementia,

and as far as I can tell there is nobody else who can drop everything and be there for her."

"Fine. I'll call you if we need you. FBI will be lead anyway, if they ever get here."

"Marc and Bruce will be here soon, not that they're needed now, I'm sure they'll be calling in another unit since the bomb exploded."

"Not before they check to make sure there aren't any more of them." Fitz stepped back from the ambulance doors to allow the paramedics to close them. "Keep your phone on, Hall. I don't care what the hospital staff says."

Justine's head felt like it was being crushed in a vise. She slowly opened her eyes, but the brightness caused her to close them again.

"Hey, my super special agent, are you awake?" he whispered.

"Where am I?"

"In the hospital."

"Which one?"

"Abrazo West Campus."

"What happened?"

"You may know the answer to that better than I do."

"I don't remember."

"It happened so fast, you were on your phone, presumably with your boss. The next thing I knew an explosion rocked the area and you were pinned under a flag pole. Give it some time. It'll come back to you."

"An explosion." Her hands reached for her head. It felt like the throbbing intensified, though she doubted it was possible. "Is everyone okay? Were they evacuated in time?"

"Don't you remember? They evacuated immediately when the threatening call came in." He reached for her hand.

"I can't recall any of it."

"You will. Give it time."

She wondered why he'd come. It wasn't like they were a couple. He'd only been out with her twice. They'd shared a few kisses, but he didn't owe her anything. She tried to search his eyes for answers, but came up empty.

He squeezed her hand. She'd take it. It felt comfortable for him to be there. She couldn't explain it, but he belonged by her side.

"Can I get you anything?"

"Water would be great."

He poured some from the pitcher on her tray and handed it to her.

She drank deeply. "I think my head is going to explode."

"We've had enough explosions for one day."

"I hear you."

"What's wrong with you that makes you want to work with live explosives?"

"A great many things. Do you want a list?"

"Yes. That will be your homework when you're well enough to complete it."

Justine hung up the telephone after calling the nursing home. "I'm not sure they understood why I couldn't bring my mother tomorrow, but they agreed to do her intake on Monday. I'm supposed to be back in Virginia by then, but considering my day my boss will understand if I take an extra day or two."

"He took two of your days for work, so he owes you that much," Brady said.

"How about you explain that to him?" She yawned and stretched.

Brady stood. "I'll let you get some rest."

"Can't you break me out of this joint." She whispered.

"Not tonight. We'll see what we can do in the morning."

Marc appeared in the doorway. "Hello, doll. I see you're not hurting for company." He slid a sidelong glance toward Brady.

"Hi, Marc. You missed the excitement," she said.

"So, I heard. You got yourself blown-up. I knew you needed me for more than my handsome face."

"I didn't get myself blown-up. From what I understand, I was a little closer to the blast than was healthy, but the EOD suit did it's job and I'll be fine."

"Glad to hear it. You gave us a scare. How's Lindy?"

"Brady took her home with him and Blitz. She wasn't hurt."

"Good to hear."

"You need help getting packed up here, so you can get back to Virginia?"

"No. I didn't bring much and it looks like I'll be here a few more days."

"For what?"

"I still have to get my mother into the home."

"Can't her nurses take care of it."

"It's something her daughter should do."

"What about your siblings, can't they do it?"

"I'd rather do it myself."

Brady approached the bed. "I'm going to take off. Call if you need me."

She smiled and squeezed his hand. "Thanks."

Turning back to Marc, she asked. "What's this about? Why the rush to get me back to Virginia?"

"There is no rush." He leaned closer to her. "I miss you. I

miss us."

"We can't keep having this conversation, Marc." She tried to sit up straighter, but failed. "There is no 'us' anymore."

Marc sat in the chair beside Justine and watched her. She wondered if they'd ever be able to get back to the friendship they'd once had back before they'd decided to take a chance on a relationship doomed to fail.

Once inside, Brady slammed the truck door. Who was he kidding, he couldn't compete with a guy like Marc Jackson. Words washed over him, not audible, but clear as a bell. "You don't have to compete. Be yourself."

He took a deep calming breath, and drove toward home, talking to God as he did. By the time he'd arrived back at the ranch house, he'd made a decision. Justine wasn't going to leave town without knowing how he felt about her. He wouldn't simply say the words. He would show her. Real men put actions behind their words.

Heading out his back door, he watched as Blitz and Lindy ran together, played together, and herded animals together. It was bittersweet. For them, there couldn't be a happily ever after, Blitz belonged to the Arizona Department of Public Safety and Lindy belonged to the FBI. Training dogs was expensive, and neither department would allow an exceptional dog to retire early. If he moved to Virginia to be near Justine, Blitz would be forced to stay here and be assigned another partner. The thought hurt, but the idea of a life alone hurt more and Justine was the only woman he'd ever considered trying to make a life with. Maybe Blitz' new partner would allow occasional visits. He was thinking like a man standing on the high-dive about to plunge in. Would he slice through water smoothly or belly-flop on the surface?

He filled the dogs bowls and called them in. He wasn't up for eating after the way he'd left the hospital. Letting Marc get the better of him was wrong. She'd told him they were over, so why did he let the guy get under his skin? Going back to the hospital would be a mistake. Justine needed her rest.

A plan formulated in his mind. He'd fly out now and head back late tomorrow afternoon, if he could arrange it. She would hardly notice his absence. He picked up the telephone and left her a voicemail message, since she'd be expecting him in the morning. The desire to see her was overwhelming, but the need to find a way to give their budding relationship a chance was greater. He'd look into options in the morning. Make her believe he was serious.

Brady unfolded himself from the rental car and stretched his arms over his head trying to work out the kinks. The plane ride had been wearisome, but now it was time to enjoy a quick breakfast at Waffle House.

He opened his laptop and read through the information Grayson had sent him about the company. Now was the time to make a move. It had only been a couple of dates, but the connection was real. He felt it and he was sure she did, as well.

After paying his check, he got back in the rental and drove to the office building that housed Garrison Security. He was impressed when he got on the glass elevator. He could see indoors and out. The building was sleek and modern, glass and steel. The top three floors were rented by the security firm. When he arrived at the receptionists desk, devoid of anything, but a telephone and a computer, he advised the young woman that he had an appointment with Grayson Garrison. She disappeared into the back, returning moments later with Gray.

"It's been too long." Grayson held out his hand.

Brady shook it. "You don't have to break my hand to prove you're still stronger, Gray."

The other man chuckled. "Why don't you join me in my office. I'll have Missy bring us some espressos."

"Sounds perfect. I could use more caffeine. The flight had seemed endless."

They chit-chatted about mundane matters while they waited for Missy to bring their drinks. Once she'd disappeared from sight, Gray leaned back in his chair and made eye contact with him."

"So what brings you east to see the firm, Brady? I've been trying to drag you here for five years."

"I may need a job."

"You've got it. Can you start today?"

"I'm thinking of asking a special woman to marry me and she works and lives in Virginia."

"So what about the ranch? Your animals?"

"I don't know yet. I'm hoping I can find a property an hour or so from town that will enable me to keep the best of both worlds, but if I can't. I may still do this. Chances like this only come around once or twice in a lifetime. Isn't that what you've been telling me?"

"I knew immediately with Jenna. And wouldn't hesitate to do it all again, if I could."

"Well, I might be pushing the limits of sanity even more than you did. Your three-month whirlwind engagement was long-term compared to what I have going on."

"And what's that?"

"We met this week."

"You can't be serious?"

"A lot has happened in that short-time. Enough to allow me to get to know her. And she'll be leaving town in a couple of days. Am I crazy to be considering this?"

"Only you can answer that. Have you prayed about it?"

"Of course I have. I'm not sure of the answer though. What if I'm following my own will thinking it's His will?"

"Keep praying about it. Don't do anything until you're at peace with your decision."

"Thanks Gray. Now let's talk salary and benefits, I don't intend to work for you for a pittance like I did in college."

"We will come up with a generous salary and benefits package, but why don't you worry about getting the woman thing straightened out. I'll make some phone calls about properties you might be able to purchase."

"You're a good friend."

"I better be the best man at your wedding."

"I wouldn't dream of asking anyone else."

Disappointment threatened to overwhelm Justine when she got the voicemail from Brady. He'd called sometime during the night to let her know something had come up and he wouldn't be able to come to the hospital. She wondered what was keeping him away. Maybe it was work related.

Marc had stayed late the night before. It took some convincing to get him to head back to Virginia instead of getting a hotel room. She needed to find a way to make it clear to him she wanted to remain friends, but that anything more was out of the question. For some reason, he was making it difficult. He'd been the one who didn't want to commit. She wondered where his sudden change of heart was coming from.

She pushed her breakfast tray aside having only taken a couple of bites of cold scrambled eggs and a few sips of orange juice. Sometime soon a doctor should be by to let her know if she could leave the hospital.

A knock on the door frame got her attention.

"Come in." She adjusted the sheet around her.

"Special Agent Gillespie."

"Sir, what are you doing here? I mean, I didn't expect to see you all the way out here." She attempted to sit up straighter.

"I had a meeting in Phoenix and thought I'd drive out and see how you were holding up after yesterday's events." SSA Harrison Reed cleared his throat. "There is something I wanted to discuss with you."

"What is it, sir?" Her fingers almost twirled her hair, but she forced herself to still them. Folding her hands on top of the sheets, she took deep breaths and waited for whatever was coming.

"It's come to my attention that you and Special Agent Jackson are romantically involved."

"Not anymore, sir."

"Be that as it may, in our line of work, when emotions get involved it makes working together dangerous. We're going to need to put the two of you on separate teams. I don't want this to come across as punitive, because it isn't. I'm only concerned for the safety of every member of my team."

"Yes, sir."

"You can call me Harrison, Justine. I'm no longer going to be your boss."

Justine's heart sank. "Okay."

"This isn't a demotion. You've been recommended for a supervisory position. They're looking for someone who knows the ins and outs of explosive ordinance work, as well as working with canines. You'd be required to visit other existing field offices regularly. Phoenix, Albuquerque, Las Vegas, and Seattle are a few that come to mind, but we'll be opening another office, possibly not far from here. It's not a guarantee, but I think you'd be a superb fit and Marc agreed. However, you should know, there are other candidates in the running."

"That's amazing. Thank you, sir. I mean, Harrison."

"Don't thank me. The Acting Director of Homeland Security is the one who tossed your names in the hat. She was impressed with yours and Marc's work at the nuclear power plant and wanted you both to be considered. Marc asked that his name be withdrawn from the running."

"Why would he do that? He'd be great."

"He claims he doesn't want to sit behind a desk. Needs the excitement of working directly with the explosives himself." Harrison moved toward the door. "I'd better get going. Keep me apprised of your recovery."

"Will do. Thank you again, sir."

He nodded and left.

Chapter 5

ustine smacked her palm to her forehead. "Mom, I
need you to hear me."

"I hear you fine, dear, but I'm not your mother. We haven't
been blessed with any children."

"A little help here, guys." She directed the question to her
siblings.

Elisa shook her head, a sadness settled over her features that
Justine would give anything to erase. "I don't know how to help."

Tony cleared his throat. "You're doing the right thing, Sis."

A doorbell rang, interrupting the family meeting. Justine
jumped at the chance to escape and strode to the door. She wasn't
sure who she'd been expecting, maybe a nurse, but the sight of
Brady Hall with Lindy caught her off-guard. He hadn't called ahead
to let her know he was bringing Lindy home.

"Thanks for keeping her." She bent down to give her dog

some love.

"Feeling any better?" He leaned on the door frame.

"I'm okay." She moved aside, so he could enter.

He stood there in the foyer shifting his weight from one foot to the other and back again. "Can we talk?"

"Sure, I guess. I'm kind of in the middle of something, but I could use a break. Give me a sec, okay?"

She let her siblings know she'd be a few minutes and then returned to talk with Brady. "Why don't you join me in the sun-room?"

"Okay. Thanks." He followed her to the room with the wicker furniture where they'd shared a few intimate moments only days earlier.

"What's up?" She plopped down in a chair and put her feet up on the table.

Brady sat down on the loveseat. Leaning back, he rubbed his hands over his face.

"Is something wrong?" Justine stood and took a step closer to him.

"No. Nothing is wrong. Sorry about yesterday."

"It's not a problem. Stuff comes up." She sat on the edge of the loveseat beside him.

"Nothing really came up. I chose to fly out to Virginia."

"Well that sounds like something."

"To see about a job." Brady picked at the button at the wrist of his flannel shirt.

"I didn't know you were looking for different work."

"I wasn't."

She reached out and turned his chin, so he faced her. "Would you please tell me what is going on? I'm confused."

"Join the club." Brady took a deep breath. "This is going to sound crazy."

"If you want to hear crazy, then you should join us in the other room. My siblings and I are trying to top each other in the wackadoodle department."

"I'm sorry. I didn't know you had company. I'll come back later."

"Brady, stop. What's up? Talk to me."

"I want there to be an 'us'. You're probably going to run the other way, but I have to put it out there."

"We've only known each other a couple of days." She chewed on the inside of her lip.

"I know. I knew this would freak you out. Look, I'm going to go take a ride. Maybe we can talk later when you're not in the middle of something." Brady stood.

"Okay." She stood and walked out with him. When they reached the door, she reached out and caressed his jaw enjoying the feel of his stubble under her hand. When a muscle twitched, she kissed the spot. "Brady, I like you. Maybe too much. But I need some time."

"I understand."

"When Marc and I broke up, it was because I wanted to move the relationship forward, but he only wanted to marry a woman who would stay home and take care of him and a multitude of children. That life is not for me."

"That's okay."

"It's not that I don't want a family. I do. But I don't want to give up my career. It's a huge part of me. What I do is important. It matters to people."

"Justine, now who's rushing things? I'm asking for a chance to try a relationship. I didn't make wedding plans. But if that's what you want, it could be arranged. I hear an Elvis impersonator works on Sunday nights at the Hope Chapel two towns over." Laughter crinkled the corner of his eyes.

"Does not. And you're now winning in the wackadoodle competition."

He reached for her again and ran his hands up and down her arms. "You're an amazing woman, Justine."

"I'm not so sure about that." She took his hand in hers.

"Can I see you tomorrow? Or have I completely scared you off."

"Probably not tomorrow. We're putting my mother in the home and then we'll probably spend the rest of the day fighting over stupid things."

"Tuesday?"

"I'll be on my way back home."

"So, that's it then?"

"A wise man once told me, if we're meant to be, God will make it work. I'm paraphrasing but you get the gist of it." She leaned in, placing her lips against his.

He pulled her closer and deepened the kiss. He leaned back breaking the connection. "I'll be waiting for Him to make it work because He brought us together for a purpose greater than bomb disposal." He whispered the words against her neck.

She wrapped her arms around his neck and pulled him close again. After a minute or so of losing herself in the kiss, she pulled back. "Goodnight, Brady."

He gently brushed a strand of hair behind her ear. "I think we have something worth exploring, Justine." The way he said her name was like a caress. Brady turned to go. She wanted to call out to him to stay, but instead, she trudged back to the room where her siblings and mother awaited her presence.

The drive to the nursing home was expectedly awkward. Justine didn't know what to say. The woman who'd raised the three of them was suddenly being torn from her home and placed with strangers. Of course, to her, everyone was a stranger, most of the time, anyway. The guilt ate at her stomach leaving her nauseated.

Why did doing the safest thing, the best thing for her mom, feel so rotten? Her siblings were in her corner. There was nobody opposed to the idea, except for Mother, who didn't know anymore what was for the best.

Once at the home, Justine walked around to the passenger door to help her mom. Taking her arm, she led her inside.

The receptionist stood when they walked in. "Intake?"

"Yes. This is my mother, Mrs. Hilda Gillespie."

"A pleasure to meet you, Hilda. I'm Denise. I'm going to go get Margie and I'll be back in a jiffy."

Twenty minutes later, her mother sat in a recliner watching birds outside the window of her room. It seemed peaceful. Certainly safer for her to be under the watchful eyes of the staff of the Sunshine Home. She'd noticed most of the staff referred to the facility by the shorter name rather than the Sunshine Canyon Assisted Living Home.

A wave of sadness came over her as she said her goodbyes an hour later. It was time to head back to her mother's house and get her belongings in order. Elisa and Tony were meeting her there. Her eyes filled, but she kept the tears from falling. With a shaky smile pasted on her face, she gave her mom a hug and kiss. The smell of gardenias mingled with the antiseptic smell of the home. Justine scooted out of the room, fully expecting another sleepless night.

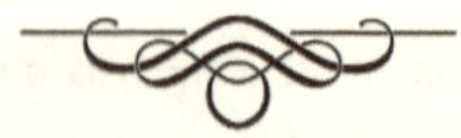

Justine's eyes were glued to the road. The night before had

been brutal. She'd lain awake until past four o'clock fretting over mother's move. She'd taken an early flight. Now she was driving to Quantico in near white-out conditions. This definitely hadn't been part of her plan when she'd left Arizona.

She shifted her focus to work to keep from fretting about the roads. Since she wasn't an investigator, her involvement in cases was limited in scope. This one was different, it was personal. They'd nearly sent her to meet her Savior. Although she longed to meet Jesus, leaving like that would devastate her family. Choosing such a high-risk career made sense when she'd done it. Now she wondered if it was time for a change. She could have a shot at a supervisor slot. If she was offered the position, it might be a sign that it was time for a change.

Lindy whined from the seat beside her. Reaching out, she scratched the dog behind her ears. She'd need to stop soon if the roads didn't improve.

Brady Hall invaded her thoughts for the umpteenth time as she neared her destination. There was something about him that made her think about white picket-fences, as corny as it might be. The ringing of her cell drew her attention away from her reflections.

"Hello." She answered her cell and Brady's voice came through the car speakers.

"Justine. It's Brady."

"Hi."

"Our office got a phone call. I thought you guys might want to take it."

"I'll be back to my office soon, so I can call you when I arrive, or if you'd prefer, you can call SSA Harrison Reed and give him the information now."

"All right. I'll do that."

"Okay. Thanks," Justine said.

"Thanks. I'll talk to you later." Brady's voice was clipped and professional.

Justine gave him Reed's number and disconnected the call. Something felt wrong. She'd followed protocol. It wasn't her case and Reed would get it to the investigators, but her gut told her something was amiss. She pulled into the lot and grabbed Lindy's leash.

Brady stared at his cell. It was obviously over between them. Justine had sounded distant and cold. He'd used the call as an excuse to speak with her, so he could hear her voice. A mistake.

He picked up the office telephone and dialed the number Justine gave him for Supervisory Special Agent Harrison Reed. The FBI sure liked their titles. The man answered on the first ring.

"SSA Reed."

"This is Trooper Brady Hall with Arizona Department of Public Safety."

"How may I help you, Trooper Hall?"

"We received a call from a concerned power plant employee asking about our investigation on the recent bombings. Since it's your case too, I wanted to pass it along."

"Thank you for the call. I'll make sure the information gets to the investigators."

He gave the name and telephone number of the concerned employee to Reed and promised to send the recording of the call. He'd thought it odd that the employee who'd received the threatening call was informing them instead of the FBI, but maybe he didn't know the investigation was being handled by the feds. It was even stranger that the call came through Fitz' desk line instead of the dispatcher, but that happened from time to time.

Brady took a sip of bitter black coffee and nearly spit it out. It seemed they were always out of cream. Maybe he should learn to like the powdered stuff. It would be easier to keep on hand.

Once outside, Brady realized the rain was coming down hard now. They were going to have a busy patrol ahead of them. Stormy nights were rarely dull. Hopefully, he'd have time to stop for a coffee before dispatch started hassling him.

Walking in high-heeled shoes through six inches of snow hadn't been what Justine had in mind when she'd left her mother's house that morning in the sweltering heat. The nor'easter had been on everyone's radar, but it had been expected to hit farther north, near New York City. Her plane had left Arizona before the storm hit Virginia and nobody had expected them to get hammered. The temperatures were cold enough at thirty degrees for the sustained snow-fall to accumulate. It was a miracle her plane had been able to land.

Once inside the front-doors, Justine advanced through the metal detector and tried to shake as much snow off her shoes and slacks as possible. This day was shaping up to be a real winner.

She took the elevator up to her office and connected her laptop to the port. It was time to get some paperwork done. Before long, there was a rap on the door frame. Marc.

"I wasn't expecting you back so soon. How are you feeling?" He asked.

"I'm okay. The doctors say I had a minor concussion. My other injuries weren't bad either. They were concerned about internal damage, but the tests came back fine."

"Wonderful news. Did Reed talk to you?"

"He did. He mentioned you'd withdrawn your name from the running. Why?"

"We need to be on separate teams, doll. I'm too distracted by your presence to keep working with you. I'm the one who told Reed we were involved. When he mentioned the supervisory gig it seemed perfect for you. I don't want to stand in the way of your career. Other opportunities will open up for me. This one will allow you to be closer to your mother."

"You did that for me?"

"If you tell anyone I've gone soft there will be repercussions."

"Don't worry, my lips are sealed." She stood and gave him an awkward hug. "You know I care greatly for you."

"I can't hear the 'let's just be friends speech from you'. Please don't. I saw how you looked at him. I'm stepping out of the way."

"Looked at who?"

"Don't play stupid, doll. You know who. Kill the interview and get the job, so I won't have to see your pretty face around here."

"I'll try."

Marc's eyes lingered on hers a moment longer before he turned and left her office, patting Lindy's head on his way out.

She felt empty. Marc had been her closest friend, well human friend for several years. There were no girlfriends to speak of. The FBI bomb squad was a boy's club and she'd somehow made it in. Time outside of work was severely limited, so she didn't have time to socialize. Her sister, Elisa, was the only person other than Marc she spoke with regularly. Her heart ached. Getting involved romantically with a friend had been a huge mistake.

Laying her head against the back of her desk chair, she closed her eyes. Her day wasn't improving. The tears couldn't be held back any longer. Hurrying to the door, she locked herself in and slid down the wall to a sitting position. There on the floor, she sobbed. Lindy licked her face and snuggled up close reminding her that she still had a friend.

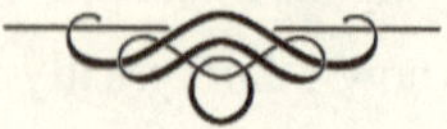

The call came in from dispatch that a trooper needed assistance. They'd gone to speak to a suspect and he'd taken off into the woods behind his home. Brady turned on his lights and headed to the location to provide backup. Turning to his partner he patted the dog on the head. "We've got one for you, Blitz, a runner to chase down."

Blitz' excitement made it clear he understood. He loved his work. They arrived on scene ten minutes later.

"Hey, Kearney. We're under a flash-flood warning. Where did your guy go?"

"He went that way." Kearney pointed in the general direction of the dry river basin. "They asked me to bring this guy in for questioning. I knock on the door. He sees the uniform, flips out, and runs."

"Do you know what you were questioning him about?"

"Well, yeah. They were going to ask him about the bombings. I don't think he's even a suspect. A witness."

"He's a suspect now."

"Sure is."

Brady grabbed a shoe from the pair sitting by the door and gave it to Blitz to get the man's scent. He felt bad for Blitz having to smell the guy's stinky feet. It didn't take long for Blitz to pick up his scent. Not even five minutes passed before Blitz found the guy hiding in a cave along the riverbank.

"Come on out of there, so we don't have to come in and get you."

"Call off your dog."

"I already did, but I wouldn't try to run again if I was you. Come on down."

"Why'd you run?"

"No reason."

"You ran for no reason?"

"I, uh, I didn't want to talk to cops."

"Why?"

"I don't have anything to tell them."

"Fine. Let's go. You have the right to remain silent. Anything you say, can and will be used against you. You have the right to an attorney. If you cannot afford an attorney–"

"I know my rights."

"One will be appointed–"

"I said I know my rights."

Brady finished reading the guy his rights and put him in the back of Kearney's SUV.

"Are they going to get a warrant on this guy's place?" Brady asked.

"I don't think running is probable cause. Fitz will have to

find something on him first."

Brady climbed up the stairs to the guy's porch and looked in the filthy window. "I think you have your probable cause. Looks like a meth lab. We're going to have to evacuate the area. Does it ever end?"

"It does not." Kearney took off his hat.

"I guess we know now why he ran."

Kearney peeked in the window. "Looks like a meth lab, all right."

Five hours later, Brady sat at his desk writing his report with Blitz at his feet. The smell of wet dog filled the station. Fitz strolled past. "Hey, Fitz. What did meth guy have to do with the bombings? Was there a connection?"

"It turns out that first bomb threat, the hoax originated from his house. We were simply trying to figure out if the first one was related to the others and it appears they are. The second two were made from a burner cell purchased locally with a credit card in his name, Chris Connell."

"Huh. So, is he responsible for what happened to Justine?"

"It's a definite possibility."

"That sounds definitive." Brady laughed.

"He might be a patsy for someone else. We don't know yet, but we're holding him. FBI will take him tomorrow for further interrogation."

"I hope they get answers."

"We all do."

Justine stared at the ceiling. Sleep evading her once again. As exhausted as she was, nothing should be able to keep her awake, but nagging thoughts wouldn't let go. After two hours of tossing and turning she gave up and brewed a cup of tea. She tried to read, but the words blurred together. Picking up her cell, she sent a text. "Are you up?"

"Leaving work."

"At 12 a.m.?"

"It was a rough night."

"Can you call me when you get home?"

"Yes."

She stared at the 'yes' on her screen for the ten minutes it took for her phone to ring. When it rang, she jumped at the sound. "Hello."

"Hi, Justine." His tone was different than usual. More business-like.

"Thanks for calling."

"Did you need something?"

"Yes. I wanted to hear your voice."

His tone softened to a caress. "You did. Well, then, I'm happy to oblige."

"That's better. You seemed off when I talked to you on the road this morning and again when you just called."

"Sorry, I thought you were trying to blow me off this morning."

"I wasn't. Driving in a snow storm had me on edge and I wanted to make sure I was following protocol."

"My mistake. Forgive me?"

"Of course."

"We may have caught someone involved in the bombings tonight. He's being turned over to the FBI, so you should be able to get more information than I have on him."

"Really? Nobody's called me. I guess they won't though. It's not my case anymore."

"They don't share information?"

"They're pretty tight-lipped for the most part," Justine said.

"Well, he doesn't appear to be a sophisticated bomber as much as a meth distributor who samples his own product. Boss man thinks he is someone's puppet, but getting that information could prove challenging."

"The FBI has their ways." She drew out the words in a sing-song voice.

"I'm sure they do." He chuckled.

"Can we talk about something else?"

"Sure, anything. What's on your mind?"

"I want to see you again."

"You do?"

"Yes. I do. I have an interview at the Phoenix field office on Friday, can I see you afterwards?"

"I would love that. I'm on the schedule, but I'll get someone to switch shifts."

"Then it's a date?"

"It's a date."

They talked for another hour about a myriad of topics, simply enjoying the lingering conversation.

Chapter 6

Justine's heel caught on the curb as she climbed into the driver's seat of her rental car. The interview had gone well as far as she could tell. Having five interviewers pepper her with questions was a bit intimidating, but she'd held her own. The rental car smelled like shoe polish and fake pine scent. A strange combination, that oddly enough made her think of Marc. He was forever polishing his work shoes and kept one of those pine tree air fresheners in his car. She couldn't stand the smell of fake pine and would much rather open the windows for a fragrance no air freshener could match.

A buzzing in her purse let her know she was getting a call. She dug around until she found it. "Hello."

"Hi."

"Hi, Marc."

"Wondered how it was?"

"I think it went well."

"Are you coming back tonight? A few of us are getting to-gether after work."

"You made it crystal clear you didn't want to remain friends and didn't think we should see each other. Not even around the office."

"I know. I just–"

"It's okay, you know. I'll survive without you."

"Are you sure you're okay?"

"I am."

"The other day you didn't appear to be taking it well."

"I'm all right. Goodbye, Marc."

"See you around, Justine."

She hurt, but thought it better to let the friendship go than to keep reopening wounds. A clean break was better for both of them.

Putting her ringer back on, she tossed her cell in the console. She had a long drive ahead of her, but it would be worth it to see Brady. Her mind made a connection she immediately wanted to undo. Considering her recent break-up with Marc, Brady would be the rebound guy. She didn't want Brady to be a rebound relationship.

Flipping the radio to a southern gospel station, she sang along to the hymns as she drove back to Tonopah. It was an attempt to keep her mind occupied, but it was only half working.

Justine pulled up at Brady's house. Sitting in the car for a few minutes, she tried to gather her thoughts. Knuckles rapped on the window. She jumped at the sound. Lowering the window, she smiled. "You scared me."

"Sorry about that. Why are you sitting in your car?"

"Thinking."

"About?"

"You."

"I like the sound of that. Do you want to come in?"

"I'm not sure that's the best idea. Are we going to head out?"

"I'll behave myself if you come in for a minute. I need to say goodbye to Blitz and grab my jacket."

"Okay. I'll come in."

She sat on Brady's couch and stroked Blitz' head. Lindy was back in Virginia with another agent. Normally she'd have left her with Marc or brought her along, but this trip was a solo interview and Marc was no longer an option. "So, where are we going?"

"Shouldn't you be deciding that, since you asked me out?"

"I, uh–"

"I'm kidding. I thought we'd go to Marley's. They have fabulous crab-cakes and you mentioned you like them."

"I do. That sounds delicious."

"I know I said I'd behave, but..." He pulled her to her feet and close to his body. Lowering his head until his lips met hers he kissed her gently. She deepened the kiss not wanting it to end.

When he pulled away from her she tried to breathe evenly.

"Now we should go. Otherwise, I can't be held responsible for what happens next."

"I'm pretty sure you'd still be responsible."

"Then we'd definitely better get going."

"Brady?"

"Yes?"

"I don't want you to be my rebound guy."

"Perfect because I don't intend to be."

"What do you intend to be?"

"I guess you'll have to stick around long enough to find out."

Brady held the restaurant door and waited for Justine to walk inside. He mentioned their reservations to the hostess who promptly took them to a booth along the window. He took her hands in his while they waited for the food.

"You do something to me no woman has done before."

"What's that?"

"You make me think about a future with you."

"You're crazy. We've talked about this. We've only known each other a short time.

"I know. But, when you know, you know."

"What about the rebound thing?"

"I'm not worried about Marc. You weren't in love with him. It's obvious when the two of you are together."

"What makes you think I will fall in love with you?" She let a smile play at the edge of her lips.

He leaned closer. "Are you trying to crush me?" He whispered.

"I wouldn't want to do that."

"I know you feel what I do."

"And how do you propose we make a long-distance relationship work?"

"I'm still working on the details. I've got the job thing worked out, but moving the ranch won't be as easy."

"You can't do that yet."

"I'm not going to. We'll have a few more dates first."

"A few?" She choked on her water and sputtered, "are you serious?"

"Yes. I am. I know what I want and I intend to get it."

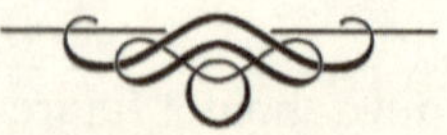

Dinner was delicious. Justine savored every bite. And the company was nearly perfect. Until he'd brought up the future. Was he seriously considering rooting up his life for her? She couldn't let him do that. It wasn't fair to him. And what about Blitz. Blitz belonged to DPS, they weren't going to give him up easily.

Justine's heart ached. How could they ever make it work? Maybe this job interview would pan out. They'd talked about having her work out of the Phoenix field office or even possibly opening a satellite office in Buckeye. She could commute to and from Phoenix from her mother's house, but it would be a long drive. If she could work from Buckeye it would be ideal. If, she got the job, that was. It was a big if. It wasn't like she was the only candidate. They'd interviewed several other qualified agents.

"What are you thinking about?" Brady reached over and took her hand in his while he continued driving back to his place.

"About that interview I had this morning."

"How did it go?"

"I'm not sure yet."

"What's it for?"

"A supervisory position."

"Wow. That's quite a promotion." Brady squeezed her hand.

"It will be if I get it." She sighed.

"I'm sure you'll get it."   ·

"I hope so."

They pulled up beside her car and he came around to open her door.

"Thank you for tonight, Brady."

"You're welcome. It was great. When can we do it again?" He took her hands in his.

"I don't know yet." She pulled her hands back.

"Don't run away from this. I know you're scared and freaked out by the timing and the whole rebound thing, but I can tell you have the same feelings I do. Don't let fear ruin this. Promise me you'll pray about it."

"I will. I'll definitely pray about it."

"That's all I can ask."

She leaned close to him and put her head on his chest.

His arms closed around her and he held her for several minutes before walking her to her car. "I would invite you in, but we both know it would be a bad idea."

"Yes, it would," she said.

"Are you staying up here tonight or flying back to Virginia?"

"I'm going to stay at mother's house and I'll fly home in the morning."

"Text me when you get there, please."

"I will."

He kissed her gently this time and she didn't deepen the kiss because she didn't know how to keep the flood of emotions that accompanied his kisses from overwhelming her. The drive home to her mother's place left her filled with anticipation for the next kiss she would share with Brady and the hope that he would be the one. The man she could fall in love with. If she hadn't already.

Brady dialed Grayson's number. "Hey Gray, did you talk to your realtor friend yet?"

"I did. He has a few properties for you to look at. I told him to email them to you."

"Oh. Great. I hadn't checked my email. I'll do so now."

"How's the girl?"

"Justine? She's great. Not a girl. A woman."

"And does she know she's the one yet?"

"I'm trying not to scare her off, but I'm failing. I think she's thought about running more than once."

"Don't be too intense. Take your time. She'll come around if she's the one."

"She's the one."

"You've prayed about it?"

"I have."

"Has she?"

"I asked her to last night," Brady said.

"What did she say?"

"She said she would."

"Maybe she is the one," Gray said.

"She is. Her faith in God is strong. I think she's struggling some because of what's happening with her mother, but she's a believer."

"Wonderful. There is nothing more important for a relationship. Two cannot walk together if they are not agreed."

"You'll get no argument here. I've tried it with other relationships."

"Yeah, me too. I'm glad I married a believer," Gray said.

"I wouldn't dream of doing otherwise."

"Let me know what you think of the properties he sent you. Jenna and I can tag along while you tour them if you want."

"Will she make me some of those cookies?"

"You definitely need your own wife."

Brady chuckled. "That I do, but not for cookies. I'll call you later."

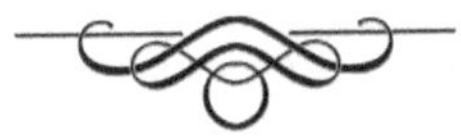

The call offering Justine the job came early Monday

morning. There was nobody to celebrate with. She told Lindy, who perked up her ears slightly, but was otherwise disinterested. "The job is for you too, girl. You could show more enthusiasm."

They hadn't made a final decision about the location for the office, but the possible locations were all within an hour of her mother's place. She picked up the telephone to call Brady, but changed her mind. This was the kind of news he would want to get in person. Maybe she'd take the next couple of days off and fly back to Arizona. She was in-between assignments at work, so she had nothing worthwhile to do in Virginia anyway.

After packing her bags, Justine called a cab to take her to the airport. Lindy jumped in to the passenger seat and looked far more excited than she had been at the news they'd gotten promoted. It seemed as if Lindy knew where they were going and was quite pleased about it.

When their plane landed, Justine rented a car and headed straight to Brady's house. She swallowed her disappointment. He wasn't home. Maybe she should've called first. He was probably working.

She shot him a quick text. "Where r u?"

"Work. Everything okay?"

"Yes. Can you call when u get off work."

"Will do."

After driving to her mother's house, she settled in on the couch with the remote in her hand and Lindy cuddled up beside her. They binge watched Netflix while they waited for Brady's call.

Several hours later her cell rang. "Hello."

"Hi. What's up, princess?"

"Are you done work?"

"I am. I'm headed home now. Why?"

"Do you think you could come here instead?"

"To Virginia?"

"No. To my mother's house."

"You're here? In Arizona?"

"In the flesh."

"I'll be there in ten. I'm not showered from work yet."

"That's fine."

"Just so you know, I would've come to Virginia if you asked me to."

Brady pulled up to Justine's mother's house. He reached into the glove compartment and pulled out a pack of gum and some deodorant, so he could freshen up some. He ran his fingers through his hair to remedy the hat head and ambled up to the front door, Blitz at his side. A moment after he rang the doorbell, Justine opened the door and flung herself into his arms.

"This is a welcome surprise." He whispered against her neck.

She leaned back slightly grinning from ear to ear. "Hi."

"Hi, yourself." He traced the outline of her jaw with his thumb. "You're in a jovial mood."

"I am."

"Want to let me in on what's got you in such a great mood?" His cell rang and he glanced down at the screen. "I don't want to answer this."

"But you have to. I'm in law enforcement too. I get it."

He took a few steps away and answered. "Trooper Hall speaking."

"Brady. We've got another one."

"Another what, boss?"

"Bomb threat."

"Really? I thought we were done with those."

"This one is far more personal."

"How so?"

"They're claiming they have bombs in five of our stations."

"If that's true, we're talking five bombs."

"Exactly. We don't have enough teams available to handle this. I'm calling in the FBI again."

"I'm with Justine. Maybe she can get you to the exact people who need to be involved sooner rather than you going through bureaucratic red-tape."

"Perfect. What are you doing with Special Agent Gillespie at this time of night? Never mind, I don't want to know."

Brady handed the telephone off to Justine and listened with a growing admiration as she asked questions and then made phone calls to coordinate a response.

When she finished her phone calls, he pulled her close to him for a brief kiss. "I guess I'm headed back to work."

"I'm coming with you."

"I'm sure Fitz wouldn't have it any other way."

Justine set up a staging area on the local flea market grounds. It became a place for local, state and federal law-enforcement to coordinate the efforts to assess the threat and determine a suitable course of action. She'd gotten the clearance she needed to take Lindy to the nearest DPS station to sniff out explosives. She hoped it was a hoax, but something in her gut told her there was more to it than that.

Brady drove her and Lindy to the station. She did something she'd never done before. Forgetting caution and professionalism, she kissed Brady without worrying about who was watching. "I intend for Lindy and I to make it out of there alive and when we do, we plan to make a life with you."

"Are you trying to tell me something?"

"I'm falling for you, Brady Hall. I don't want to get near any bombs without telling you how I feel first."

"The feeling is mutual. Hurry back. I'll be waiting."

"I'll do my best, but it's up to Lindy how quickly we clear the building."

She let herself out of the truck and allowed Lindy to lead the way into the station. Justine found herself jumping at every sound. Maybe she wasn't ready to do her job again. She had been through a traumatic event whether she wanted to admit it or not. Lindy did her job efficiently, while Justine followed her from room to room. When they'd cleared the building, they made their way back outside. Brady was waiting by the door.

"You were supposed to wait a safe distance from the building."

"I know."

"Yet, you completely ignored the directive."

"Sure did."

"Lindy didn't find anything. Looks like a hoax. Or possibly a diversion to keep law enforcement occupied." As the words left her mouth, her phone lit up, as did Brady's.

"Las Vegas. They found a suspicious package," she said.

"Airport."

"FBI is sending a jet here with the bomb squad. We'll get them diverted to Vegas. I'll make the call."

He leaned against the building and pulled out his phone as she made the call.

After disconnecting her call, she turned to face Brady. "Was that Fitz you called?"

"It was. I gave him your update," he said.

"Thanks. Are they going to move back inside?"

"I believe so."

They sat around the conference table at the station, waiting on word from the Las Vegas police. It surprised Justine to learn that Marguerite was a nail biter. She and the other woman spoke on and off throughout the night. Maybe they would become friends. She could use a girlfriend and she was growing fond of Marguerite, despite her initial impressions.

When the call finally came it was from Marc, rather than from the Vegas P.D. "Justine, doll, we've found it. Stan did a little acid magic and he's removing it now." Her face grew warm at the endearment. She should've told him he was on speaker-phone. The grins on the faces of the others sitting around the conference table didn't ease her discomfort. Brady reached over and squeezed her hand under the table.

Thank you, Jesus. They still needed to clear the rest of the stations to be on the safe side, but it looked like another disaster had been averted. In the process, she'd learned she didn't mind being on the coordinating end instead of standing next to the bomb. Her new job as a supervisory agent was waiting for her and she was ready to embrace the change.

Brady drove them to another nearby station which Lindy promptly cleared. The DPS bomb squad checked the other sites. By the time the four of them arrived back at her mother's place, Lindy and Blitz were pooped. They both collapsed on the floor in the den and she and Brady sat together on the couch.

"So, as I was saying earlier. I have some news." She gazed into Brady's eyes.

"What news is that?" he took her hand and turned to face her.

"I was offered a supervisory position."

"That's great. Congratulations." He squeezed her hand.

"It would allow me to stay here. My commute would be an hour or less depending on where they put the office."

"Are you serious?"

"I am."

"I knew you had an interview, but I didn't know it could mean you'd stay."

"Would that please you?" she asked.

"More than anything. I was prepared to uproot my life to follow you to Virginia, but this is more than I could ever hope for. It's the best of both worlds. God is awesome."

"That He is."

"Justine?"

"Yes?"

"I'm falling in love with you."

"I thought so."

He pulled her closer. "You did, huh?"

"I did. Because the feeling is mutual. I love you, Brady Hall."

He kissed her with a passion he'd been holding back, but forced himself to separate from her a few minutes later.

"Are you ready to think about forever?"

"Soon," she said.

"I'll take it." He nuzzled her neck, placing tiny kisses along her throat and up to her ear. "I need to get out of here before I lose control."

She put her head on his chest. "Before we lose control."

"Yeah. Before we do. It's late our boundaries could get blurred."

"I could see how that could happen." She held him tighter, making no move to separate.

"Walk me to the door?"

"Sure." She forced herself to move away from him. She glanced over at Blitz and Lindy who were curled up together in front of the heating vent. "Who is going to tell Blitz he has to leave?"

"I guess that's my job." Brady called his dog who gave him a disgruntled whine before joining him at his side.

Chapter 7

Brady got down on his dog's level and looked him in the eyes. "Now, pay attention, Blitz. This is serious. Do you think March 31st is too soon for a wedding? April 1st is Resurrection Sunday and I would love to celebrate it as husband and wife. We can have a double wedding with you and Lindy."

The dog tilted his head and placed his paw over his snout.

"I'm not sure that qualifies as an answer. I'll have to ask Lindy."

Blitz yawned and closed his eyes.

"Fine. Be that way." Brady stood and made his way to the kitchen to make some coffee. Once again, he would have to make do without cream.

A sound outside caught him off-guard. He wasn't expecting anyone. Moving to the door he watched as Justine let Lindy out of the car, while balancing two coffee cups.

He opened the door. "This is a pleasant surprise."

"We were in the neighborhood." She held out a coffee to him.

"You are an angel."

"Not quite."

"I was out of cream. Again."

She smiled.

"Did you hear from your boss?" He asked.

"About?"

"The bombers."

"Not yet."

"Turns out it was the supervisor of the guy who got the call at the nuclear plant. That was supposed to be their big showing, but you thwarted their attack, so they had to regroup. Thus, the bomb at the school to make us take them seriously. And then the false threats as a diversionary tactic. They could've exploded a bomb in Las Vegas Airport. Can you imagine the devastation if they'd succeeded?"

"Well, praise the Lord they didn't," she said.

"Amen."

"Are you working today?" She reached for his hand.

"Not if I can help it. It's supposed to be my day off and I ended up working a double yesterday, so..."

"So, you're free to spend the day with me?" She swung his

arm with hers as they walked toward the kitchen.

"Absolutely. I need to feed the animals first."

"I'll help."

They spent the next forty minutes feeding and playing with the animals. Having her there felt natural. Comfortable.

They sat close together on the bench overlooking the river watching the birds flit over the surface.

"So, are you going to marry me? Or do I have to wait a designated amount of time?"

"How can I marry you when you haven't asked?"

He reached into his pocket and pulled out an engagement ring. It was a princess-cut diamond set in white gold. He'd noticed she wore more silver than gold and thought it would match her existing jewelry.

Getting down on one knee he held the box out to her. "Will you marry me, Super Special Agent Gillespie?"

"Are you serious?" She opened the box. "It's gorgeous."

"Are you going to leave me down here in the dirt? Or are you going to answer my question?"

"I'm probably crazy to agree to this already, but, yes, I'll marry you."

He joined her on the bench and placed the ring on her left

hand. "You've made me a happy man."

"Even though you thought I was mentally unstable when we met?"

"I haven't ruled that out yet, but I'm in love with you anyway."

He drew her to him and held her tightly for several minutes before standing and pulling her to her feet. He kissed her as the rain began to fall. When they finally separated he noticed she was soaking wet and shivering. "Shall we head back to the ranch?"

"March 31st? Are you insane?" Justine paced the kitchen of Brady's ranch house.

He relaxed against the counter. "I'm impatient. Not insane."

"How can I plan a wedding in seventeen days?"

"You didn't want a huge wedding, did you?"

"No. But, I do want my family there. And I want to get married in the church. Wait. Can we get married at your church? I attended a Bible church in Virginia, but I don't have a church near here. My mother was rarely a church goer. She took us to Catholic services for Christmas Eve and Easter, but she didn't take religion seriously."

"Is she born-again?"

"I don't know. I heard her claim to be once, so that's what I cling to. She has so few moments of clarity these days. It's hard to find a time to bring it up."

"How about we head out to the home now? I'd love to meet her."

"Now?"

"Why not?"

"Okay. If you're sure you want to meet her already."

"I am. I'd love to meet your siblings too."

"That proves it. You are insane. Full scale wackadoodle." She leaned over to poke him in the chest.

He chuckled. "If Pastor Dan can marry us on March 31st, will you agree to the date?"

"Yes. I will."

"I'll make sure he includes a salvation message, for both of our families."

"Sounds perfect."

"You're the best. You know that?"

She smiled. Her smile could light up the darkest corner of the earth.

He left the room, cordless phone in hand. "Brother Dan?"

"Hey."

"How's your schedule on Saturday, March 31st?"

"I'll be fretting over the Resurrection Sunday sermon. Why?"

"I'm getting married. Can you marry us?"

"That's awfully sudden, isn't it?"

"When you know, you know, right?"

"If you say so."

"She's the one, Dan. Can you do the service?"

"I'd love to. She is born-again, correct? Please tell me she's saved."

"She is."

"Great. It's settled. Are you going to have the service at the church?" Pastor Dan asked.

"Yes. Definitely. There is one more thing."

"What's that?"

"We'd like it if you would include a salvation message and altar call. Can you do that?" Brady asked.

"Nothing would please me more. Can you two come in after Sunday service for premarital counseling and planning?"

"I have to check with Justine, but I think we can. Pencil us in and I'll call if we can't make it."

Justine was suitably impressed. Brady was so sweet with her mother. It was a bad day and yet, he handled it with practiced ease. On the way to dinner he reached for her hand. "You know, we could move your mother in with us after we get married."

"It's kind of you to offer, but I'm not sure you want to take on the responsibility of caring for someone with dementia. She isn't going to get better."

"I understand. We dealt with it with my grandmother."

"I don't know. I hate having her in a home, but I think it's the safest place for her. Why don't we revisit the idea in a few weeks?"

"Sounds like a plan."

When they got to the Tonopah Inn and sat down to dinner with her siblings, Brady was charming and funny. He held his own in the conversation. That's when she knew he would fit in with her family. It was a relief.

"Where have you been hiding him, sis?" Elisa asked.

"I haven't been hiding him. We haven't known each other long."

"Sure. And you're getting married? My sister who plans ten years of her life at a time. I'm not buying it."

Justine laughed and Brady reached over and squeezed her hand. They would let her siblings think what they wanted. They knew the truth. Tony monopolized the conversation with talk of baseball spring training. Brady knew enough to keep up. Overall it was an excellent day and she felt ready to marry him. She was anxious. Unsure if it was too soon, but she was also delighted.

Lying in bed that night, a thought occurred to her. She needed a wedding dress. She got out of bed and scurried up to the attic. She knew her mother had kept her wedding dress for her and her sister to wear if they so desired. She found it packaged up in a big white box. The dress fit her nearly perfectly. It might need to be taken in slightly around the ribcage, but her sister was handy with that kind of thing, so she'd get her to take it in. She twirled around in front of a full-length mirror and then she added the tiara wrapped in the box with the dress. As she was putting the dress away, she noticed a paper folded up in the bottom of the box.

> If you're reading this without me, I want you to know I hope if you wear this dress, it will be on one of the most amazing days of your life. I pray you are as in love with your future husband as I was with your father. May every moment of your lives together be savored. I sit here today watching my two daughters dance around the living room in ballet slippers while their brother tries to trip them. I know time will march on and you won't always be children, so I am penning these words, so you will know you are my joy and my life, even if I'm not there to remind you. You are your father's pride. Please know whatever the future brings, we will always love you.

> -Mother

By the time she put the letter down, tears streamed down her cheeks. Her mother had thought ahead. Prepared for the possibility she might not be there for these special moments. She never could've known it would be dementia that would rob her of her memories, essentially leaving them without her guidance. Yet, her thoughtful words had given Justine what she needed. Reassurance. It was going to be a life worth living with Brady by her side.

The day before the wedding was chaotic. Having a small wedding was supposed to make it easier, but the details seemed endless. Justine made them a list and split it in half. She took half for herself and left him the other half. He was supposed to make sure his vows were memorized, the caterer had everything they needed, the flowers arrived at the church hall, the place cards were in their proper places, and he remembered his steps for the first dance.

Sounded simple enough, but getting in contact with the caterer proved difficult. The flowers hadn't yet arrived. The place cards were not where they belonged. It was proving to be a much harder list of tasks than he'd expected. When Gray walked through the doors of the church hall, he wanted to shout with joy. Someone he could unload some of these tasks on had arrived.

"Grayson, so glad you're here."

"You look panicked."

"I am," Brady said.

"Take a deep breath."

Brady followed the directive.

"Let me see your list," Gray said. "This isn't so bad."

"That's what you think. Wait until you try to accomplish the tasks on that list."

"I'll take care of everything except place cards and vow

memorization. You already know the dance, so cross that off."

"How do you know that?" Brady asked.

"No woman in her right mind would let a man wait until the last day to practice their first dance."

"Why don't you go spend a some time with God and come back in here when you're ready to face your few remaining tasks? Somehow I don't think your panic has anything to do with this list." Gray held the list up in the air and waved it at him.

"You may have a point. I'll be in the front of the church if you need me."

Brady sat in a pew near and stared at the wooden cross. He poured out his heart to the Lord and a peace settled over him. This marriage would work because they would both put Jesus first. As long as the Lord remained their focus, they would be in His will and that was the best place to be.

The tiny pearls around the bodice of her dress matched the pearls in her tiara. Her sister had curled her hair and pinned it, so waterfall curls cascaded from a twist on top of her head. She'd never felt more beautiful. The fragrance from the jasmine in her bouquet comforted her as she walked down the aisle. Her eyes met Brady's and she could see the appreciation in his gaze. His tuxedo fit him well and she longed to embrace him.

Her sister was her matron of honor and Brady's friend, Grayson, was his best man. Lindy and Blitz stood beside them. They'd kept the wedding party small.

At Pastor Dan's directive, they read their vows and exchanged rings. When Brady bent down to kiss her, she struggled to breathe. She was overwhelmed with love, so much love for Brady.

Once they made their way to the foyer to greet the guests, Pastor Dan preached a message of salvation and played "Just As I Am" for the altar call. Justine watched through the window on the door as several people moved toward the front of the church. Her heart filled with joy. She gazed up at Brady, grinning. What better wedding gift could there be than to see family and friends receive Jesus as their savior on their wedding day.

Brady pulled her away from the door and kissed her thoroughly. All was well in her world. They weren't planning a trip right away, but they intended to start their honeymoon immediately. Justine was grateful to God for this new love. Tonight, she would be lawfully held by Trooper Brady Hall and she intended treasure him forever.

Dear Reader,

I hope you enjoyed reading my romance novella, *Lawfully Held.* Please check out some of my other titles, including my debut novel, *Stella,* the first book in my Endless Mountain series. The second book in that series, *Claudia,* released on December 15, 2017. The third and final book in that series of stand-alone novels is *Sofie,* which will release later this year.

If you enjoyed *Lawfully Held,* the most helpful thing you can do is leave an honest review. So, please consider submitting a review on Amazon and/or GoodReads. It doesn't cost anything, other than a moment of your time and can be tremendously beneficial to me. Your quick review helps to get my book into the hands of other readers who may enjoy it.

https://www.amazon.com//dp/B079Y861CK

https://www.goodreads.com/book/show/38751760-lawfully-held

For a list of my current books and upcoming releases check out the novel page on my website:

https://www.elleekay.com/novels/

Thank you.

Elle E. Kay
https://www.elleekay.com
https://www.lawkeeperseries.com

About Elle E. Kay

Elle E. Kay lives in the Back Mountain area of Pennsylvania. She loves life in the country on her little farmette. Elle is a born-again Christian with a deep faith and love for the Lord Jesus Christ. She desires to learn how to live for Him and to put Him first in everything she does.

She writes children's books under the name Ellie Mae Kay.

You can connect with Elle on her website and blog at https://www.elleekay.com/ or on social media:

Facebook: https://www.facebook.com/ElleEKay7

Twitter: https://twitter.com/ElleEKay7

Pinterest: https://www.pinterest.com/elleekay7/

Google+: https://plus.google.com/u/0/+ElleEKay

Amazon Author Central: http://www.amazon.com/author/ellekay

Instagram: https://www.instagram.com/elleekay7/

Goodreads: https://www.goodreads.com/author/show/15016833.Elle_E_Kay

To join the Lawkeeper Series mailing list, please sign-up at https://lawkeeperseries.com/newsletter

To view the other books in the Lawkeepers series, please visit our Amazon page at:

https://www.amazon.com/The-Lawkeepers/e/B079MNY47R/

Acknowledgements

I would like to give special thanks to my husband, Joe Kelleher, who took the time to read my work and make suggestions. He put up with me and my hectic schedule over the past few weeks. Thanks also go out to my fellow Lawkeeper Authors who invited me to join the series. I'm happy to be a part of the group.

This story is a product of my imagination. Any similarities to actual events or people are purely coincidental.

Any errors or deficiencies are my own.

Coming Soon

the next book in the Lawkeepers Series

LAWFULLY ADORED

by Jenna Brandt

A K-9 Lawkeeper Romance

Police officer Aiden O'Connell looked out over the mountain peak at the setting sun and knew only a small window of time remained to find the missing hiker.

Aiden was bent down next to his German Shepherd partner, Cooper, allowing him to inspect an area below a cluster of towering pine trees between a set of giant boulders. True to his trained behavior, Cooper barked and urged Aiden to follow him up an overgrown hiking trail.

Clear Mountain, Colorado was a popular destination for tourists. The craggy rock formations overlooking the quaint town were a constant attraction for outdoor enthusiasts, but often inexperienced hikers would underestimate the dangers of the area, causing themselves to get hurt or lost.

Aiden and Cooper were one of the only two K-9 search and rescue teams for the entire area and the Clear Mountain Search and Rescue team compromised of only five officers total. The constant call-outs to the surrounding mountain areas kept the unit busy.

This evening, a wife of a missing hiker came in from Boulder to report her husband hadn't returned home after his weekend hiking trip, resulting in the team being deployed to locate the missing man.

"K-9 2, this is K-9 1, we aren't having any luck over on this side. What's your status?" a deep male voice echoed out over the radio.

Aiden pulled the receiver for his radio free from his dark blue uniform and pushed the button on the side to talk back. "K-9 1, we might have gotten a possible beat over here." Pulling a map out of his back pocket, Aiden glanced down to confirm his location, still getting used to the area after transferring from Boulder County Police a year prior. "We're two clicks from Meadow Ridge near the cluster of pines by the twin boulders."

"Copy that, K-9 2, we're headed over your way." Like a well-oiled machine, Cooper and Aiden continued to move up the trail with Cooper stopping every few hundred yards to inspect a new area. The west side of the mountain sheered off, leaving only forest on the east side.

Several minutes later, a second German Shepherd came charging in from the right side of Aiden and Cooper. The smaller dog joined Cooper and playfully nipped at him while the same male voice from earlier said, "I think Harley is jealous of Cooper for picking up the scent on this one."

Aiden turned his head to the right, recognizing fellow officer, Zach Turner. "Eh, it's only cuz Cooper has a couple of years on Harley. She'll catch up soon enough, especially with you handling her Zach."

"Yea, but I was hoping to find this hiker on my own so I could finally secure that date with that female reporter from the Clear Mountain Gazette that keeps following you around."

Aiden shrugged. "Me and you both. It would be great if you could get her off my back."

"Man, what is it with you? Have you seen her? She's hot; a solid nine. What? Are you holding out for a ten?"

"No, she just seems more attracted to the badge than to me and you know I'm not into that," Aiden explained.